TWISTED

Tales

Short Fiction and Poetry by
the Infinite Monkeys Chapter
of the League of Utah Writers

INFINITE MONKEYS

Twisted Tales

— Short Fiction and Poetry by the Infinite Monkeys Chapter of the League of Utah Writers

Anthology Copyright © 2025
by The Infinite Monkeys Genre Writers Corporation

Individual works are Copyright © 2024 by their respective authors

ISBN-13: 978-1-7325836-8-9 (Paperback)
ISBN-13: 978-1-7325836-9-6 (Ebook)

Library of Congress Control Number: 2025906733

Edited by:
    Danielle Harward, Talysa Sainz, Johnny Worthen & Dan Yocom

Managing Editor:
    Talysa Sainz

Layout by:
    Johnny Worthen

Cover design © 2025 The Infintie Monkeys Genre Writers
Cover design by RebeccaCovers.

Contents

What Are Our Twisted Tales

Daniel Yocom

Twisted tales come in many varieties. There are classic tales with twisted endings—popularized by authors like O' Henry. Twisted fairytales are another story format—currently stories like Wicked are popular. Switching out characters from a known story to provide a different point of view—Ghost Busters with a female cast. And genre mashups combining two or more genres that bring us stories—like Cowboys and Aliens. Some stories are just twisted in our way our thinking.

The League of Utah Writers Infinite Monkeys Genre Writers also come in many varieties. Our styles cover all the aspects of different genres of reading. Above the ideas of the genres we write in is our love for telling stories. Finding the setting where the story lives many times takes us to the fringes where one genre collides with others. Places where our stories can take on a new life of their own.

We work in these secluded backwoods of storyland. Our hope is to create an experience for our readers. New stories take on a life of their own where they can transport a reader to a new world, even if it is a place we are familiar with. Stories that feel familiar are given a new place to live where the telling allows all of us to see things in a new light. We, as the writers of these stories, want to create a connection with you, as a reader, and make a bridge where the story becomes something more.

The members of the Infinite Monkeys are a tribe of storytellers who work alone and in collaboration to create new tales for the enjoyment of creation.

In Twisted Tales, you will find the familiar and the new. There are characters you already know while others will become new friends. The characters live in places where their stories can be told, and all of us can find pieces of relatability. And being respectful of who we are as a collective, this collection covers many genres.

I invite you to join us on this journey through time, space, and to new worlds. We will travel across the genres: some you have already experienced and others that may be completely new to your reading palette. Working with this wonderfully creative crew of writers, I enjoy the wide variety of talent and styles. I hope you find selections that entertain and inspire. May you also find new authors you enjoy.

On behalf of the authors in this anthology, we thank you for joining our characters on their travels as their stories unfold. We hope we spark your imagination and inspire you. We invite you to join us in more adventures, either in person or on the page. Most of all, we hope you enjoy our writing of our twisted tales.

Daniel Yocom
President of the League of Utah Writers Infinite Monkeys Genre Writers Chapter

How Gods Die

Jacob Badger

A front-row seat to the end of the world.

That was the joke Immortals shared anytime one of their cloned bodies was decanted. Whether that joke was a threat, a warning, or a promise is left up to the individual Immortal. For some, it's an overblown cheer that they've cheated death, and will continue to do so until the clock runs out. For others, it's a weary reminder of the centuries behind them and asking if it's worth it to continue the ride all the way to the end of the line. Others still take it more literally, like there will be this great meeting with all the Immortals and old gods where everyone will pull up a chair, a snack, and a drink to watch the fireworks. Whether all hell will break loose, and the angels and demons run amok, the warriors of mythology will rise from the dead to do battle, or if all the stars simply wink out one by one, anyone who survived the long winding trek of eternity would be treated to one last show.

Perhaps that was why Eric Vesper was sitting in the living room of his massive penthouse apartment as the city of Chicago burned around him. He even had a plastic bottle of Mountain Dew on his armrest and a bowl of genuine movie popcorn with real butter on his lap as he pulled up to watch the show. Holographic screens showed police, rioters, soldiers, and combat bots duking it out from every major city on Earth as the lights of fire and the sounds of gunfire echoed from the streets outside.

Every protester wore the black and luminous white war paint

that depicted a glowing human skull. The war paint of the Reapers. They had declared all-out war on the wealthy Immortals who feared death and the decadent society that propped them up. And by the looks of the riot police and military buckling under their advance and the stolen and hacked military transport and combat bots they brought to the party, the Reapers were winning.

A front-row seat to the end of the world.

And here was the end of the world.

And yet through all this chaos of this apocalyptic present, Vesper's mind was still focused on the past. Vesper himself was born at the tail end of some great pandemic in the early twenty-first century. His mom would often joke about how almost every day there was some new catastrophe, and the entire world was laughing at the absurdity of how much was going wrong at that time. But he had the solid childhood, loving parents, and siblings he loved but also couldn't stand, he went to school, and made a few friends, the usual stuff that kids did in those days.

But the life he was remembered for really got started when he joined his first band in high school.

Vesper may not have been the best student; average grades would probably be the best descriptor. But as soon as he met his fellow bandmates in the school cafeteria, he became that student who was always skipping class to play in his friend's garage. It was a decent set up too, with pretty good soundproofing and a couple of fire extinguishers that they, thankfully, never had to use.

Vesper wished the movies about them being musical geniuses, writing hit after hit with every strum of a guitar was how it actually happened. But the truth was, they started off exactly how everyone else started off. Terribly. He tried for a month to get as lost in the sound as his fellow bandmates, but he was just way too embarrassed by the number of covers they butchered.

Then one night after another session of seeing how many rock and roll legends they could make spin in their graves, something clicked.

Vesper couldn't play any instruments worth a damn at the time, but boy could he sing. He was simply messing around with a few poems and lyrics, and then something just…happened. He started singing about running out of time, trying to keep up with an ever-changing chaotic world. He was so lost in the lyrics that he didn't even notice his band trying vainly to catch up with him. He didn't fully realize what had happened until he finished the song and the rest of his bandmates applauded. He had to go back through the video to catch all the lyrics, but soon enough they had a proper demo of the song that they uploaded to YouTube just for fun.

That was how their first single, Race Along the Edge of a Knife, became a viral sensation.

It wasn't quite the overnight success people like to paint these things to be, but it came pretty close. Soon other singles were released for the web, and people from all over were offering them gigs to play before a live audience. They had all skipped out on their own graduation for a gig in Salt Lake City. They got Hell over that, but that show was worth it.

Of course, Vesper's father hated him being a singer and a rockstar. Vesper wasn't sure if his old man's disapproval stemmed from his son wasting his life, or the fact that his son now made more money than he did.

But it didn't matter to Vesper. When he was on that stage, people loved him. He had found something he could offer the world. And every time he sang out to the crowd, the same thought circled in his mind.

If only this could last forever.

That was about the time when Human Clone Insurance companies really got started.

Vesper heard about it the same way everyone else did. A YouTube ad on his phone when he was looking for music videos. At first, he thought it was that immersive advertisement for some sci-fi blockbuster that was coming out, but sure enough, after conferring with the rest of the band and a couple of Google searches, they came to the conclusion that it was all real.

An old-declassified DARPA project that allowed Black Ops fighters to cheat death and keep fighting was now made commercially available to the public. Technology had caught up with the dream of human cloning, and now it was on sale for everyone to give it a try. Even some of the retired Black Ops soldiers decided to invest and endorse the same technology that brought them home.

To be fair, it wasn't advertised as a way to cheat death or to live forever back then. That drama was still a century down the line. The program the insurance companies offered was marketed as a second chance, a backup in case of an accident or a mistake. In the old days, if you were struck by lightning, hit by a car, or conked your head and drowned, then that was it. The story was over, and you were used as a cautionary tale before they even had the decency to put you in the ground. Now, you would just wake up and move on with your life, grateful for the miracle of a second chance.

And there were many job fields where that second chance was accepted. First responders like the policemen and the fire department leapt at the chance of still being able to go home to the family even after the worst should happen.

Of course, there was pushback against clone backups, especially from the religious and the spiritual. The Christians, Jews, and Muslims hated it because it allowed soulless corporations to play god, and the Hindus and Buddhists hated it because it mocked reincarnation. Vesper's father was a fire and brimstone Baptist, so he was as closed-minded as they got.

Not that Vesper really cared. He was a singer in an up-and-coming band; he'd never have enough money to buy a clone backup for himself. And his bandmates were in the same boat as him. They saw it, they thought, would be nice, like driving a Maserati, but it was never going to happen, and moved on with life thinking that was the end of it.

Vesper had almost forgotten about it until one of their bigger fans, a rich oil heiress turned carbon capture baroness, came backstage after one of their shows. They could tell she was loaded by the black dress with fancy white fur on the edges and the very cool holographic dragon that danced around her neck. Not to mention the black-suited bodybuilders in sunglasses that followed her in.

But despite being a woman dressed like she was on her way to a royal ball, she was a super fan. She knew every lyric, she had every song downloaded, and even had You Can't Stop Us Now as her ringtone. Not even Vesper had that song on his phone. They spent most of the night chatting like she was a fellow member of the band.

Then she dropped the bomb that would change their lives forever. "Have you ever heard of LifeCycle Assurance?" she asked.

Of course, they had heard of it. It was the largest clone insurance company at the time. Every week, there was some tabloid reporting about a new protest turned ugly outside of a LifeCycle building or a new celebrity buying a spare clone from them. It was the premier cloning service with a price tag so obscene that Vesper and his band could never afford it in their wildest dreams.

Guess what their biggest fan had just bought the entire band. "Just in case," she assured us, like those words didn't mean what they did.

Anyone who has worked in or around the cloning industry knows full well what "just in case" entailed. Just like everyone in the band knew when the baroness gave us the paperwork for the insurance policies and left. They were too stunned to say anything after that.

But the gigs, then the tours went on, and Vesper stopped thinking about it. He didn't cancel the policy. That seemed rude. He continued his life and never thought about there being another him in a jar somewhere, waiting for a tragic accident. He was simply happy to be touring with his band and singing his heart out for the world.

Then he got in his first car crash.

One minute Vesper was driving a supply run for pizza and beer, and the next he was waking up naked on a gurney covered in amniotic fluid and gasping for breath, like a drowned man pulled from the water. The only difference between his old body and the new body was a bar code on his right arm.

His friends called to see if he were decanted. They shared footage of the wreck and how totaled the car was. Thankfully, they never shared what happened to his first body. That was a nightmare he was thankful to never be haunted by.

The doctors called him lucky.

He didn't feel lucky seeing footage of his death while sitting on a hospital bed and coming to terms with his new body.

That's when it struck him like a car running a red light.

He didn't have to worry about death anymore.

His father wouldn't take the news so well.

Vesper knew he had to tell his family eventually about him being on his second body. His bandmates kept hashing on him to just come out and tell them before they found out about it in a tabloid.

The problem was you couldn't stop by for a Sunday dinner and say, "Hey, Mom, I'm a clone now, can you pass the mashed potatoes?"

Vesper had the whole thing planned out. He would drop by when the band wasn't touring and surprise them on Easter. Looking back, it may have been in poor taste to announce he had been resurrected on that particular holiday. He would talk to his mother first, then his sister and her husband, and finish off with his father and take off for his next tour. It was a good, solid plan.

Unfortunately, his father beat him to it.

They were sitting down for dinner when his father asked about the car crash. Naturally, his mother and sister were concerned, asking him what happened and if was he okay. But his father only glared at him like he'd broken an antique vase and was waiting for his son to confess to it.

He knew.

Vesper showed them the barcode tattoo on his wrist.

Everything went wrong after that.

His mother covered her mouth in horrified shock, and her sister who could always be counted on for an inappropriate joke didn't say a word. Vesper respected her choice to avoid a confrontation, but his father wanted one. Sensing the coming scene, Vesper fled the house. His father, however, caught up to him in the driveway and tried to turn him around, earning 600 volts from his son's security jacket. Vesper had heard horror stories of soldiers being attacked by their families and even getting shot for coming out as clones. So, he came prepared. At least the shock jacket gave him some room to try and talk his father down from his homicidal rage. But his father refused to talk it out. He'd shouted, "I didn't take you to church every Sunday for twenty years so you could piss your soul away!"

Vesper's right hook broke his jaw, which was something he never felt ashamed about. The fall to the concrete however broke his father's knees. That he did feel ashamed about.

He paid for his father's hospital bills, but once everything was settled, they never spoke again. Vesper went on tour with his band in Europe, and he thought that would be the end of it.

Later Vesper learned his father had neither forgiven nor forgotten it.

He was in Japan when the small article became a big global headline. An article called, Meet the New Gods, Same as the Old Gods. Reference to the Who aside, the article was completely unapologetic clickbait written by a sensationalist hack named Delilah Vane.

The beginning part of the article was rather interesting, summarizing the myths of different gods. Many stories showed that Zeus was a serial rapist and Hera was a toxic wife taking her jealous rage out on hundreds of other women. There was a story of how Thor kidnapped and press-ganged a pair of children for the crime of eating the bone marrow of a goat Thor killed and brought back to life as a crippled animal. Even a story about how the great sun god Rha was so old and senile, that when the people of Egypt questioned him on whether he was still a fit ruler, he created a murderous lion woman assassin and unleashed her on Egypt.

Basically, her point was that the gods of old could do whatever the hell they wanted because they had all the wealth, all the power, and they were immortal. So, what mortal could ever hope to hold such beings accountable for their sinful actions?

There was one quote that underlined the theme of the article perfectly that even centuries down the line it was still crystal clear in Vesper's mind.

Now that human cloning has allowed the wealthy and powerful to cheat the great equalizer, society is now at risk of creating an overclass with all the Divine ability of the gods of old, with even less of the accountability.

The coup de grace of the whole thing was his father's two-page rant about, "the abomination that stole my son's life!"

There were days when Vesper wished he hadn't turned down the in-person interview, just so he could curse that hack out to her face, that self-righteous, sanctimonious, mother f…

A flaming hovercraft flew past the penthouse window, spinning all the way to the street below. Vesper calmed his raving heart, but thinking about that article, thinking about how many Reapers quoted that article in their speeches, was enough to make anyone's blood boil.

Three days after the article came out, Vesper's mother called him with news that she had divorced his father. His sister called to see how he was taking the news. It was hard to tell whether she accepted her brother being a clone, but thankfully she never held it against him.

Thankfully, she had news of her own. She was pregnant. Naturally, when the tour with the band dropped them off stateside, Vesper came by to check on his sister. No problems with the delivery, and the baby was a nice and healthy baby boy.

That was how he met his firstborn nephew.

He kept touring, kept writing songs, but he made a point of stopping in once in a while to check in on everyone. He was making more than enough money to pay off the old LifeCycle Assurance policy, so he had a couple of clones on ice if he ever needed them. He even traded his body in for a younger model to help his sister with the kids when he visited.

Vesper was clearly the favorite uncle, playing with the kids and bringing merch from his tours and souvenirs as gifts. He even got his nephew a guitar, and his bandmates were kind enough to teach him a few tricks.

Vesper couldn't remember if it was his nephew's eighteenth or nineteenth birthday when he broached the topic of adding his sister, brother-in-law, and nephew to his insurance policy. While his sister didn't scream or shout or any of those cliches, she gave him a firm no. Apparently, one life was enough for her. Vesper respected her decision. Even when she was diagnosed with inoperable cancer, he respected it. He didn't try to talk her into accepting one clone, he didn't pressure her husband to sign her up. There were times he wished he did though.

He and his bandmates attended his sister's funeral and gave their well wishes. His nephew pulled him aside to ask about the insurance policy. Vesper never pressured him, simply laid the option and said it was his if he wanted it.

His nephew simply said, "If one life was good enough for Mom, then one life's good enough for me."

He visited his nephew every year on his birthday and steadily watched him grow older.

And older.

And older.

Until his nephew became an old man.

Vesper couldn't believe the vibrant rock-and-roller nephew he'd known since he was a baby was now a liver-spotted, wrinkly geezer requiring an exoskeleton in order to walk. He put on one brave face as all the grand- and great-grand-nieces and nephews gathered around to watch him blow out the candles on his cake.

The next day, his nephew didn't wake up.

His name was Jace Isaac Veyron and he was one hundred twenty-four years old at the time of his passing.

It was a lovely service when they laid him to rest. Vesper gave the eulogy. But when they buried his nephew alongside his mother and his wife, Vesper searched the grieving crowd for any familiar face. Sure, he had gotten to know some of the younger relatives, but there were so many that were complete strangers to him.

That's when he realized that his still mortal family had passed him by. Life went on, yet here he was, a fixed point that refused to move on with them.

That was when Vesper stopped going to the family reunions.

As Vesper looked back on his life, he had to admit It was still a well-lived one, all things considered. Even after the band he started his career with broke up, there were still plenty of other bands wanting his talent. He hung around other Immortals sharing their thoughts on living forever and those they left behind. That was when he started hearing "a front-row seat to the end of the world," but he paid it little mind. He had a comfortable life, with more money than he could ever spend, and kept his clones at the ready for his centuries of active lifestyle. He would always trade them in when the early signs of arthritis started rearing its ugly head.

Yet despite that indulgence, he was never seen as one of those snooty Immortals who sneered at the proletariat for getting blood all over the hood of their brand-new Ferrari. He was seen as someone who got welcomed to the upper crust through sheer talent alone. A modern Orpheus welcomed to Olympus to party with all the gods.

It wasn't just the musical scene either. He spent decades being a producer, a teacher, an advocate, an award-winning author, and even several decades as an eccentric police consultant. That was a fun thirty years and very significant for his fellow Immortals.

It started when the son of an Immortal stockbroker committed suicide. Vesper did some business with the stockbroker and noticed that he wasn't acting like himself since he decanted into a new body. And not in the my-son-just-died kind of way either. Turned out, the kid hacked his dad's clone insurance account and switched consciousness with his old man to get the inheritance that the kid felt was owed from an old man who refused to die. After the whole thing was sorted, that case made a best-selling book.

It was hard to imagine almost seven centuries of life. How much the world had changed since he started singing in that garage. He had traveled to other worlds, seen the sights of the universe, and even played his music at the edge of the cosmos. But something—maybe it was nostalgia, maybe it was homesickness—but something would always draw him back to Earth.

Then about fifty years ago, Vesper started noticing the problems.

Some political activist calling himself Azrael started appearing all over the holonet. Mostly it was speeches about unfairness, the problems of the modern world, and how the Immortals had essentially ruined everything by refusing to die when their time came and went. Azrael always painted his face, so it looked like a skull with a black background. This was complemented by his black hooded robe.

It was really subtle for the guy who named himself after the angel of death. The only things missing from his outfit were the scythe and the pale horse.

But he was good at speaking, and it wasn't long before he had a proper following. Thousands and then millions of the dispossessed and disenfranchised flocked to his banner. They were intoxicated by his message of hatred towards Immortals, and the promise that they could change the world for the better. The followers painted their faces like their messiah who ran their little outfit like a cult.

It started with traditional protests, crowds gathered outside cloning facilities, hospitals, and government buildings waving signs and holographic banners with catchy slogans. These were usually escorted away by police or hosed down if things got really nasty. But regardless of how many times they were shooed away, the Reapers, as they took to calling themselves, kept coming back.

A few years later, the Reapers graduated from protesting to bombing. Clone facilities, genetic research, hospitals, social and political benefits, private schools—if an Immortal gave the place money, visited, sent their kids, the Reapers bombed it. Martial law was declared in the wake of the bombings and it was brutal.

It was hard to say whether the crackdown helped slow the problem or speed it up. Many Reapers were arrested, but many more of the desperate and angry joined after every one.

Yet despite their overall goals, the Reapers never seemed like a genuine threat. Year after year, not a day passed without a news story at least mentioning them, protesting, bombing, or taking hostages. But that was simply background noise to a society of Immortals that had stood the test of time and seen annoying insects like these come and go. What few friends Vesper had made among the Immortals all believed this strife would burn itself out in another couple of decades.

Then three days ago Azrael died in a police raid on his compound.

That was the spark that started the fire Vesper was now watching from his apartment. Years of build-up, of secretly amassing military hardware, hacking through secure firewalls to turn the weapons of the state against itself—all let loose in one final strike to avenge a martyred wack job.

Yet this is how gods always die, isn't it?

The barbarians at the gates have had enough of being looked down upon and treated as lesser. And thus, they break down the gates to lay low the high and mighty.

As he looked back on his long and eventful life, he came to a clear conclusion. He had regrets, sure. He wished things had been different for his father. He wished he had more time with his sister and his nephew. And even though the long centuries had exhausted him, he looked back and saw a life worth living. If that life was meant to end tonight, who was he to argue any differently?

Huh? Had he made peace with himself?

Huh.

He always assumed there'd be more to it than that.

Soon enough, Vesper heard the sizzling crackle from his front door and noticed the blue lights that sparked across his tiled floor. He watched the plasma carver cut a hole through his reinforced apartment wall. His door was locked and barred, so anyone who wished him ill needed heavy-duty equipment, and, apparently, they had it.

His Reaper execution squad had found him.

Vesper drew in a deep breath, gently stroking the large plasma pistol with high high-capacity fuel cell in his drink holder. He had no illusions of fighting his way out, but he would go happy taking a few of those skull-faced terrorists with him. As the plasma cutter continued sawing through the wall, Vesper clicked the plasma pistol on.

With a single electric whirl and a simple blue light, he was ready to smite those who defiled his home.

That was when he heard the plasma fire from the hallway as the cutter stopped. The weapons fire intensified and then suddenly fell silent. That silence seemed to last for a century even though it was only for a few moments.

His lock beeped as if someone was entering the code. But the only ones who knew that code were…

The door opened and Vesper shielded his eyes from the light outside. He blinked and squinted to see…the police?

Yes, the Chicago Police Department armed to the teeth securing his now damaged doorway. He saw all the Reapers that had attempted to storm his apartment lying dead across the hallway floor.

Vesper sighed as he holstered his pistol and spared one last look at the burning city behind him. For all the centuries he had lived, and all the bodies he wore, his tired old soul may yet have a few centuries left in him.

A front-row seat to the end of the world.

Maybe it wasn't a guarantee, but right now to Vesper, it felt like a promise after all. His end may come someday, but not today.

French Fried

Sobey Snow

Pete Potato had been standing in the freezer aisle for the last five minutes, pretending to decide which kind of breakfast biscuit he wanted, but what he really had his eye on—what he really craved—was reflected in the glass. Right there. A few feet behind him, behind another glass door, in a slick, golden package fit for a showgirl not afraid to dance in the limelight, French fries.

This was it. He'd been pumping himself up for weeks. Preparing, mentally, for the risk he was about to take. Ever since the war against the humans. Ever since the root cellar, his hunger for them has been insatiable. They'd peel him apart if he got caught. Cannibalism, they'd call it. But... but... they're so good. And he was ready.

When no one else was in the aisle, he turned around, yanked open that chilly, see-through door, and... oh, darn. Did he want Regular? Curly? Crinkle cut? Steak cut? Seasoned? Did he want Soft? Did he want Crispy? Decisions, decisions.

Too many decisions.

An approaching shopping cart squeaked as it rounded the corner. Too late.

"Oh, hello, Peter."

"H-hi Mrs. Raisin." His breath huffed out in front of him.

"What are you up to?"

"Huh? Oh. Nothing. Just some fries fell down, is all. If it was me, I'd appreciate if someone sat me back up straight, is all."

"You are a sweet potato. Well, I'll take a bag just for you."

"Of course." Pete began to pull a bag of Regular fries out of the freezer.

"I prefer the curly ones. They're fun, aren't they? I'll bet those potatoes had quite the personality in life. Don't you?"

"Yeah," Pete sighed. "I wonder which one I'll be when my timer's up?"

"Oh, dear." Mrs. Raisin laid her hand on his round back. "Regular's just as good."

He dropped the bag of Curly fries in her cart.

"Thank you, dear. Tell your father to give me a call. It's been a while since we got together."

"Yes, ma'am."

As she turned the corner and the aisle was clear, Pete snatched a bag of Regular fries. Because Regular is just as good.

He stuffed them under the peas and carrots already in his shopping cart. His heart beat to a rhythm of both excitement and fear. He glanced right. Glanced left. No one. Feeling like he'd just buried a body, he took a deep breath to calm his nerves, the way he did when nightmares from serving in the Edible Revolution woke him up at night.

He left the frozen foods and headed straight for the self-checkout, getting in line behind some pop-tart who was leaving sprinkles all over the floor.

Familiar faces surrounded him: Mrs. Raisin, Berry Muffin sagging his wrapper, O.J. picking at his expiration label. Were they watching him? Did they know? No. No, of course not. How could they? Unless Mrs. Raisin really did suspect something? Oh man, you never can trust a raisin.

"Sir." The attendant waved at Pete. "Checkout two is open."

Pete pushed his cart over and started scanning his purchases. Slow is smooth, smooth is fast, he told himself. Slow is smooth,

smooth is fast. A phrase he'd overheard a human say once on the battlefield and it stuck. It didn't work out so smooth for the human... but that was beside the point.

The line trailing him produced exaggerated sighs. He was a burglar under the spotlight.

When he got to the sinful bag, his hands shook. The frozen package sounded like his friend, Crackers, when he would walk down the aisle of the movie theater.

Pete relied on his bulky body to hide his precious prize. He scanned the fries and slipped them into a brown grocery sack with the peas and carrots. The package was secure. What a relief.

He pulled out his wallet. His palms were sweaty and still shaking. But now it was okay. Exhilarating, even.

He slid his debit card into the machine. INSUFFICIENT FUNDS popped up on the screen. The burglar alarm in his brain rang.

The line at his back was growing into an angry mob. All they were missing were the torches they would use to cook him. A bead of sweat dripped into his eye. Burning.

"What's the holdup?" A soft, muffled, but no less angry voice shouted. He thought it was Berry Muffin.

"Just. Eh. You know. The ex-wife must have gone shopping again. Ha." He blinked crazily, trying to sooth his hurt eye. He must have appeared mad to his fellow citizens behind him.

He took out the peas and carrots and was able to pay. Pete pushed his cart towards the exit. Home free.

The alarm went off. And not the one in his head.

"Sir," said a glazed donut guard, "I'm going to need to see your receipt."

"Huh? Me? Uh. What?" So close. What was this donut's problem?

As if he'd read Pete's mind, the guard said, "Nothing personal, tater. We check everyone's receipts. Haven't you ever been to a grocery store?" He chuckled at his joke. The chuckle sounded personal. "Now, as I said, I'm going to need to see your—"

"Excuse me, officer. I seem to have lost my purse," said Mrs. Raisin. "Be a dear and help me find it."

"Sure," the donut said. And to Pete, "You can go."

On his way out of the store, Pete turned around and saw Mrs. Raisin, who gave him a sideways wink and popped a grape into her mouth.

The Caretaker's Greenhouse

Makayla Nielson

The greenhouse was dark and dank, but that was how the plants preferred it. Sunlight rarely entered, and if it did it would have been fought back by the dense layers of leaves and vines coating the walls and ceiling.

Their caretaker also preferred the darkness, but had to cover his hunched back in a long, black coat to keep the chill from sinking down to his hollow, brittle bones. He shuffled along between rows of overgrown boxes, using his cane to push away vines that slithered along the ground, making his way to the back of the greenhouse.

Mr. Montgomery's gnarled fingers fumbled with a frayed piece of twine, attempting to secure a purple stem to a stick lodged into a cracked pot. Once he fixed it with a tight knot, he tossed a handful of worms at the base of the plant.

The soil rolled and quaked. Black barbed roots shot up from the earth, wrapping themselves around the worms, slicing them into digestible wriggling pieces before pulling them under, out of sight. The plant's leaves fluttered as if thanking the man.

Mr. Montgomery paid little attention to this. Instead, he depended heavily on his cane to twist himself to turn his attention upward. Across the ceiling were condensed tangles of vines, swaying despite the lack of wind inside the greenhouse.

"Good mornin', old gal."

In the back corner stood an enormous, twisted central vine that protruded from the ground and spanned out across the entirety of the greenhouse ceiling. Its leaves and ivy loomed large above the plants in a protective canopy. A single bud, dried and dead, clung to the mother plant as the sole reminder of a time long past.

Mr. Montgomery opened the window nearest him and clutched a reed whistle that hung around his neck. He held it to his lips, and not a minute later, a young crow flew in. She perched herself on the algae-infested fountain that sat in the middle of the neglected space and dipped her talons in the water before deciding to dunk herself, preening her feathers.

Mr. Montgomery shook his age-spotted head and closed the window.

The vines had inched closer to the ground now, the tips of them only a meter from the oblivious crow. They twitched irregularly, like the tail of a jaguar ready to pounce.

The crow cawed and the piercing sound made Mr. Montgomery flinch. The crow took off toward the window and the vines followed after. They swatted at the bird, only narrowly missing several times before hitting its wing with a thorough whack.

The bird squawked and faltered but righted itself. It landed on the fountain once again. This time its eyes were in constant motion, focused on the plant above. A vine struck out toward the crow, and the bird caught it in its pointed beak and clamped down. The plant recoiled.

The old man sighed. Two ground plants reached up and wrapped their tendrils around the bird. It cried out, thrashing, and one wing escaped before another tendril strapped it down, squeezing the bird until it was silent.

Mr. Montgomery snatched the lifeless bird from the warring plants and offered it to the vines that hung down above the fountain. They ignored the proffered meal and rested weakly on the man's back and shoulders. Frowning, he tossed the bird to the ground and kicked it aside, where it was dragged through the undergrowth, out of sight.

He placed one hand on his knee, holding tight to his cane with the other, and lowered himself onto a stone bench covered in green-gray lichen. He stroked one of the vines and pulled it closer to his face, examining the nearest leaf. He rubbed it between his thumb and pointer finger, and a sticky, white mildew lingered on his skin.

He passed a hand over his face and his shoulders sagged even further beneath his oversized coat.

"I knew you was gettin' close. I'd just hoped you'd go after me."

The vine lifted and brushed his cheek, lingering there for a moment.

"I'll miss you, old gal," he whispered.

The vine slipped, and the plant began to hum and vibrate softly. A yellow glow emanated from the center of its last bud.

Mr. Montgomery drew in a deep breath. He shuffled over, dropping his cane and cupping his hands below the illuminated pod.

It opened wide and deposited a plum-sized seed, dark as obsidian, into the old man's outstretched hands. The glow faded, and the vine blackened and withered. The blackness stretched up the vine, into the stem, and then throughout the body of the plant, spreading across the ceiling and down its trunk to the floor. The vines became brittle, breaking apart and crumbling to the ground.

Mr. Montgomery moaned, a deep, agonized sound, and dropped to his knees, the seed still cupped in his hands. He sobbed, his tears turning to mud as they hit the ground. Then he laid himself down, cheek to the dirt, and was gone.

From the depths of the greenhouse floor, roots thick as ropes rose and gingerly cradled the old man's body, engulfing him, pulling him under and burying him before growing still.

The remaining plants began to hum and vibrate, their buds glowing in unison. They lit the damp, decaying space, turning it an eerie green. Obsidian seeds dropped to the cold ground with unceremonious thuds while their parent plants drooped, entirely drained of color. Their leaves shriveled and cracked, their stems snapped, cut down.

And all was still.

My Cup of Tea

Inna Lyon

Session #1, End of April, Dr. Day's office

"Mr. Gray?" called the pleasant voice, the same one who had answered the phone about the earliest appointment with the therapist. "Dr. Day is ready to see you."

The petite brunette with enormous artificial eyelashes smiled at Wolfgang and pointed to one of the doors in the row of other white doors. Wolfgang tried to climb out of the waiting room's deep armchair, which he had sunken into about twenty-five minutes before. He failed. His long legs flailed up, threatening to knock the nearby coffee and tea station and send paper cups and packets of sweetener flying. The soft cushion sucked his backside deeper. He liked to show up always in advance for any event and find the most secure place—the last row of desks in school and college, the farthest seat on the back of the bus and plane, the hidden love sac cushion in Leo's man cave…

He glanced at the brunette receptionist. She kept her face professionally impenetrable, but mischievous sparkles in her eyes said otherwise. This armchair was a mistake. Maybe this stupid visit was too. Wolfgang propped his hands on the armchair rests and pulled himself up. He seriously considered dashing to the street through the front door, but the appointed white door opened. A middle-aged woman in a black pantsuit invited Wolfgang to enter.

"Please, come in."

Wolfgang stepped into a spacious room after a last glance at the front door. He looked around: a crème sofa, a coffee table, two armchairs in the middle of the white carpet, a bookshelf on the left wall, and a heavy desk near the tall window.

"Please, sit down," the woman gestured to the armchair. Thank you, but no, thank you. Wolfgang sat on the sofa, not in the middle but in the corner, away from the direct sunlight.

The woman sat in the armchair but didn't sink into it. She relaxed her shoulders and leaned back. Wolfgang did the same but caught himself mimicking her and sat straight.

"Is it Mr. Gray?" asked the woman.

"Yes, Wolfgang Gray," he answered and cleared his throat. He wiggled a bit, trying to find a more comfortable position.

"I'm Dr. Stella Day. I've been a certified therapist for 15 years now. Before we start, I have to give you a disclaimer that I'm legally obligated to report if I find out during our sessions that my patient is an imminent danger to himself or others. Anything else we talk about is confidential."

Wolfgang nodded, then looked at his nails, rubbed his hands, and put them in a lock.

"You don't need to be nervous. This is a safe environment. Tell me about yourself."

Wolfgang sat back, straightened, and finally started.

"My name is Wolfgang, but you already know that. I'm originally from Germany. I moved to the US five, no, six years ago. I work as an IT developer for a big firm downtown. I love the outdoors: hiking, fishing, hunting." The last word came out quieter.

Dr. Day wrote something with her stencil on the electronic handheld device.

"Any family?"

"No, except two elderly uncles in Marburg."

"Spouse? Partner?"

"Yes, no, maybe." He bit on his cheek and look down at the

white carpet.

Dr. Day lifted her eyes with a question, "Hmm?"

"Well, a girlfriend. But I would like her to become more."

"What's stopping you?"

"She is vegan."

"And are you not?"

"No."

"Did she tell you her reason for veganism?"

"Yes."

Dr. Day put her stencil down.

"Well, then you know that many people make that conscious choice to preserve animals. Others believe the prediction of a Meat Shock in 2040; therefore, they stopped eating meat now for a better future environment."

Wolfgang nodded. "Yes, I know. Rita told me all about it."

"Is your girlfriend's name Rita?"

"Yes, Rita Red-Riding."

"So, Rita Red-Riding and Wolfgang Gray?"

Wolfgang caught a hint of a smile in Dr. Day's tone and furrowed his brows.

"It doesn't mean a thing."

"I didn't mean to imply anything," said Dr. Day in a slightly apologetic voice.

But Wolfgang couldn't stop now and continued with a heated expression.

"Other people do. It's ridiculous." He bared his teeth. "Back in Germany, I knew a guy with the last name as Van Winkle. He suffered from serious insomnia. Nothing even close to the dreaded tale. But people still laughed and made jokes all the time playing with his last name."

"Please, Mr. Gray, calm down. I apologize if I offended you in any way. Can I call you Wolfgang?"

"I'm just saying that our names have nothing to do with Brothers Grimm's overrated tale," replied Wolfgang, registering that the phrase still came in a frustrated tone. He took a deep breath and said in a more collected voice, "Yes, you can call me Wolfgang."

"Thank you, Wolfgang," said Dr. Day. "Today, we're discussing feelings and emotions, trying to understand where they come from and how to deal with them in everyday situations. Then, we will practice possible outcomes and play different scenarios."

Wolfgang nodded again. "Where do I start?"

"It would be logical to start from the beginning," said Dr. Day. "But remember, this is your session, and you only tell me what you think I need to know."

"Ok, from the beginning, you say. I met Rita a month ago, at the end of March. At work, we have a group of people who like to binge-watch horror movies on Fridays. We gather at Leo's to catch on The Walking Dead's last season that night. Usually, we order pizza and chicken wings with Uber Eats. We drink beer, smoke pot, take socks off, tell dirty jokes, and fart."

Wolfgang couldn't explain why he said what he said in the last sentence. Was it an attempt to shock her or get a mini revenge for the irony in her voice regarding their names? He didn't know, but as soon as he started talking about Leo's man cave, the memory of their first meeting flashed before Wolfgang's eyes.

That evening, Leo asked them to behave since his grandmother died last week, and he had relatives in town staying with him. One special relative decided to join them for movie night. Leo also proposed watching Stranger Things instead of The Walking Dead. The guys met both news by disappointed booing, but it was Leo's basement.

Wolfgang piled his plate with meat, grabbed a beer bottle, and occupied his favorite seat—a love sack in the dark corner.

Ten minutes into the movie, they heard high heels clicking down the stairs. Leo's relative was late.

"I'm never late," explained Wolfgang to Dr. Day, "but as soon as I saw Rita coming down the stairs, I forgave her for all the lateness for many years ahead. She was the one."

"How come?"

"She was my cup of tea—a brunette."

Wolfgang pulled out the phone to show Dr. Day Rita's image. In that picture, the gorgeous dark-haired woman in her twenties wore a white blouse and black vest. That evening at Leo's, she had a different attire. Wolfgang remembered well those noisy, tall high-heeled red boots on perfect legs. Next, a short fake leather skirt appeared with a skinny waist, full-breast bosom confined into a frivolous top tank, and finally, full Rita—a beautiful brunette with blue eyes, dark wavy hair, and fair complexion. She held a tray covered with a linen napkin.

Back in Germany, Wolfgang watched the Pretty Woman movie countless times, but he didn't think that American women wore those boots in real life. Rita proved him wrong.

All eight men look smitten and gaped at Rita. Wolfgang saw James quietly removing his wedding ring and hiding it in his pocket. Two other guys choked on their food, and one spilled his beer. Only Leo acted normal. He paused the movie and said, "Guys, meet my cousin from Trenton, Rita."

Rita smiled and greeted them in a deep, exciting voice: "Hello, guys. Leo told me about the movie night, so I invited myself. And I brought a snack." She uncovered the tray. "Cucumber sandwiches with tofu, artificial butter, and gluten-free bread. You see, I'm a vegan for ethical reasons."

Rita walked around, offering the sandwiches. James and three other guys shook their heads, "No." Leo took the sandwich and hid it on his plate beneath the pile of chips. After the first bite,

Demian choked on his, and Andrew puked on the floor. Rita looked around and noticed Wolfgang in the corner. Their eyes met. The invisible electrical charge went through Wolfgang's tensed body as Rita approached the love sac. She leaned forward, revealing her cleavage another half inch. Feeling the eyes of every guy in the room, Wolfgang picked a sandwich and took a bite.

Even a month later, he still remembered the terrible cardboard taste of that sandwich. But he concentrated on the cleavage and Rita's breasts moving up and down as she breathed. He finished the sandwich in two bites.

His following phrase, "May I have another one?" rewarded him with Rita's smile and the hateful look from his friends.

Wolfgang didn't remember the episode or how Rita ended up sitting next to him on the love sac. He remembered her trembling during the episode and him putting his arm around her shoulders. He recalled the smell of her herbal shampoo as he breathed her hair when she put her head on his shoulder. He pictured him and Rita at grandmother's funeral, rain drizzle, and him holding the umbrella above Rita. He vividly remembered them making out, kissing, and moaning in the funeral home's closet.

"What happened after the funeral?" Dr. Day's question brought Wolfgang back to reality.

"What? Oh, yes, she went back to Trenton. But we call each other every day and meet on the weekends."

"So, did long-distance relationships work for both of you?"

"Well, for a while."

"What are you worried about?"

"Rita accepted a librarian job in Phili. She starts in two weeks with Charles Santore Library."

"It's good news, isn't it?"

"Yes, I'm happy for us. But I'm worried too. You see, to have a vegan meal once a week in the restaurant is fine with me. But if we lived together, we would have more than one vegan meal a week. And I love my meat—prime rib, hamburgers, steaks." Dr. Day put her stencil and notebook down. "Rita seems to be an intelligent person. Adjusting to living together might take time. You'll have to find a compromise regarding your daily menu. I will advise you to discuss that matter before you move together. But if you have true feelings for each other, you can find the right strategy to handle your dietary differences."

"Our session is over. Vanessa at the front desk will have the printed copy for todays' session."

Wolfgang lifted his brows surprised that the session ended so soon. He shook Dr. Day's hand and walked out. With a smile, Vanessa handed him a bill for $100 charged for one hour for talking to a stranger.

Session #2, End of August, Dr. Day's office

"Good afternoon, Wolfgang," Dr. Day greeted her patient. "You skipped a couple of sessions. How's it going?"

Wolfgang occupied the same corner of the couch. His black sweater, with a small hole in the left elbow and a stretched collar, looked too big on his thin body.

"I guess it's OK. Rita moved to Phili at the beginning of May. I live in a one-bedroom apartment, but we made it work."

Wolfgang told Dr. Day that Rita brought three suitcases of clothes and five boxes of other stuff, including books, culinary appliances, a yoga mat, and weight-lifting dumbbells. He didn't tell Dr. Day that unpacking Rita's stuff, interrupted by frequent lovemaking, took them a few days. Wolfgang's cheeks turned red thinking about those days and roleplay that included a feathered mask and those fateful red boots.

"How did you two compromise about the food?" asked Dr. Day while making notes on her device.

"The first month was like heaven on Earth. On my way to work, I'd stop at McDonald's for breakfast sandwiches and order Uber Eats for my lunch. They deliver to our office all the time—Taco Bell, Wendy's, and KFC, my favorite."

"What about the meals you eat together?"

"Ah, dinners. Don't get me wrong—Rita is a great cook. Everything she would fix us was delicious: green pea patties with buckwheat, rice pasta with sun-dried tomatoes, and baked potatoes with meatless chili."

Wolfgang sighed, remembering those dinners with tablemats and candles and Rita wearing nothing but a lace apron.

"I'm glad to hear that you are happy together and things worked out for you," smiled Dr. Day.

"Well, as I said, at first." Wolfgang bowed his head and stared at the familiar white carpet. "You could've guessed, the conflict was coming. The fancy vegan dinners became more and more rare and then something else happened."

"Tell me more about it."

In an exasperated voice, Wolfgang told Dr. Day that he had to cancel his hunting trip because Rita bought two concert tickets for the same Saturday. He had told Rita several weeks in advance that on August 14th, he would be in the woods with his friends to open the hunting season, yet Rita got the tickets anyway.

"How did it make you feel?" asked Dr. Day.

"Frustrated, not heard, neglected, dismissed."

"What did Rita say?"

"She explained that the tickets were half-priced. She said that she could not imagine me hurting those little animals, and she wouldn't know what to do with the game. And went so on about red meat being high in saturated fats, elevating cholesterol, and increasing the risk of kidney stones and cardiovascular disease. And that I will die in my forties if I keep eating red meat."

"How did it end up?"

Wolfgang turned red.

"With wild sex and neighbors banging into the wall."

Dr. Day looked at Wolfgang with an impenetrable face. "I see. Intimacy is the way to temporary resolution and managing emotions, but it wouldn't solve the conflict in the long term. Did you go hunting another time?"

"No, I couldn't find my hunting license. I was upset, no, I was mad as a wolf with rabies. But I tried to be respectful and sensitive to her diet and vegan lifestyle. Until she got a mini fridge."

"A mini fridge? What for?"

"Exactly." Wolfgang blinked his eyes and bit his lip. The events of that day flashed in his mind when he came home and couldn't find his beer in the fridge. He dug through the refrigerator full of Rita's containers and bundles of fresh vegetables.

"Rita, darling, did you see my beer?" he called to his girl-friend.

Soft steps and a timid voice interrupted his beer search.

"Wolf, baby, I was going to tell you at dinner, but now is as good a time as any. I'm switching to being a raw vegan, so all I can eat now is raw food. Your beer is processed food, so it cannot be in the fridge with my food. Your beer will permeate the vegetables' spirit. I got you a mini fridge to keep your beer separately."

Wolfgang rolled his eyes, "You're kidding me, right? Vegetables' spirit?"

"Yes, raw vegetables are susceptible to already cooked vegetables."

He wondered if Rita was going insane. He did love her. Ordering different items from the restaurant menu was one thing, but keeping their food in different fridges felt simply ridiculous. He didn't know if he could continue living like that any longer.

"What's next, Rita? Raw carrots and cucumbers for dinner for the rest of my life? I wanted to spend my whole life with you. But I'm a man; I also need nutrition, protein, and red meat. And I don't care if I get a heart attack at 40. At least I will enjoy my food for the next 15 years."

Rita's eyes filled with tears. She reached to touch his hand, but he pulled away.

"Wolfgang, I don't want to force you into adopting more healthy habits. You know my reason for being a vegan and you should know how hard it is for me to be with someone who doesn't share my values. I hoped that sooner or later you would. I feel obligated to open your eyes on the truth about the meat you eat."

"The truth?" Wolfgang wrinkled his forehead, expecting another crazy statement explaining where the baby carrots came from—maybe from the full-sized carrots consummating in the dark fridge.

"Yes, there is a video about KFC and how they prepare their chickens for the slaughter. Will you watch it?"

Wolfgang paused and closed his eyes, trying to get rid of the images of that awful YouTube video. He heard Dr. Day asking, "Did you watch the video? What's it about? I never saw it."

"You are lucky," said Wolfgang with a sigh and opened his eyes. "Even I, being a hunter, got disgusted by the video. Don't watch it. It is disturbing how KFC farms treat their chickens before the slaughter." He added in a breaking voice, "The KFC farmers cut their beaks, so the chickens won't eat for the last few days and lose their feathers for easier processing after the slaughter."

He noticed his hands shaking. Dr. Day probably saw them,

too, and offered Wolfgang a tissue. "Here, here. Would you like some water or herbal tea to calm down?"

Wolfgang nodded. Dr. Stella Day pressed the intercom button on the nearby table and called her receptionist. "Vanessa, please bring me a cup of black coffee and chamomile tea for Mr. Gray."

Wolfgang blew his nose into the tissue and added, "No sugar, please."

Dr. Day nodded to Wolfgang and added to the intercom. "Vanessa, no sugar for tea."

They sat silently until Vanessa brought two steaming paper cups a few minutes later.

After Vanessa left, Dr. Day asked, "Can we continue now? What happened after you watched the video?"

"That happened yesterday. I told Rita I would consider it, but I wanted to talk to you first. I don't think I can do it. Being vegetarian is not my thing. It's…" he paused and looked at his paper cup. "It's not my cup of tea. What should I do?"

Dr. Day put her cup away and leaned back.

"The decision solemnly depends on your projected outcome. What would make you happier? Stomach or heart. If you love Rita, you might reconsider your food choices. If you love red meat, you might have to find another girlfriend. It's up to you if you want to make it work or if it's better to let her go."

Wolfgang shook his head. He didn't know the answer. But Dr. Day was right. He had to decide for himself—stomach or heart.

"Our session is over for today. Please, stop at the front desk to grab the printed bill from Vanessa. Should we schedule our next appointment in September?"

Wolfgang stood up, leaving his unfinished tea on the coffee table.

"Dr. Day, what if I want both?"

"Wolfgang, we cannot have everything we want in life. We

have to choose one or another. We make those choices every day, every minute, every second. You must make yours. Goodbye, Wolfgang."

"Goodbye, Dr. Day."

When Vanessa printed his receipt for the session, the total showed $125.

"Vanessa. What's the extra $25.00 for?" asked Wolfgang.

"That's for your tea, Mr. Grey—the one without sugar," replied Vanessa.

"But the coffee station is right here for free drinks," he pointed to the small table with a coffee machine next to the armchair.

"Well, it's free when you pour it yourself, but there is a charge when I serve it to the patients."

Vanessa shrugged her shoulders and smiled at him.

Session #3, End of September, Dr. Day's office

"Have you ever tried raw pizza?"

"Raw?" Dr. Day paused and pursed her lips. "Hm, I don't think so. Did you?"

"Yes. Twice. I ended up with diarrhea both times."

Wolfgang sat in the armchair this time and, to his surprise, didn't sink into it. The plush fabric felt soft but firm, and the bottom cushion didn't sag. He leaned back and even threw one leg over the armchair rest. He had a new red sweater and a neatly cut beard. He greeted Dr. Day, who sat in the opposite armchair with a coffee table between them, with a smile.

Dr. Day opened her device. "You look happier than the last time. Did you make peace with Rita and dietary choices?"

Wolfgang shrugged. "The first two weeks were OK. I ate salads, nuts and seeds, and tons of raw vegetables. But Rita kept going with a raw diet and juice days twice a week. She lost 25 lbs in a month. Her skin sagged and hair started falling out. She didn't have energy for cooking, sex, or exercise anymore. I asked her to stop the torture or go to see a doctor. All in vain."

"Then what?" asked Dr. Day.

"That I cheated on Rita."

"Hmm?"

"Not with other women but with food."

Wolfgang smiled. "I ate bloody steak at the restaurants and bloody hamburgers at the BBQ with friends. I went to an authentic Czech restaurant and ate tartar made with raw ground beef and a raw egg. And I went hunting with friends and ate freshly killed game. Rita was next on my menu."

"What? Wolfgang, do you recall our first meeting and my disclaimer?" asked Dr. Day hesitantly.

"Yes, of course. No worries, doctor." The sly smile escaped from his lips. "They were dreams only. I would like to continue our sessions, but I want to thank you for your advice on the choice."

"I'm glad I could help. And I will be happy to continue our collaboration. If it's not a secret, what did you choose?"

Wolfgang shrugged. "It turned out, she is not my cup of tea."

"I'm very pleased that you're leaving my office happier and healthier. If Rita needs to meet with a therapist, you can give her my number."

"I'm afraid she is not around anymore."

"Back to Trenton?"

He remembered the scene Rita made in front of the neighbors when he took her suitcases down the stairs to the arrived taxi. And his late-night bus trip to Trenton.

"I think so," he chuckled.

They shook hands, and Wolfgang went out to see the receptionist.

"Mr. Grey, here your itemized bill, but the real one as always will come in the mail a few days later," said Vanessa, and added with laughter, "and no charge for tea today."

"That's right," said Wolfgang, folding the printout. "Vanessa, are you vegetarian by any chance?"

Vanessa laughed again. "Not at all. Give me a good juicy steak and see what I can do with it."

Wolfgang's eyes sparkled. "What time do you get off work? I'd like to invite you to dinner at the steak house."

"I work until 6 p.m., and I would love to go to the steak house. Would that sound more like your kind of tea?" said Vanessa with a wink.

They looked at each other and smiled.

Thomas I. Wahl

"**D**angnabit, that red convertible is blocking my driveway again. How can those weirdos be so inconsiderate? How would they like it if I blocked their driveway?"

"Now, honey, please stop swearing. You can still get your truck out."

"Sorry, dear. It's just that the car has been parked there before. They ignored my last note."

"Maybe they didn't realize how close they were."

"Well, I saw them heading toward that rock concert at Carolyn's. How can she get away with that in our neighborhood? I am tired of all that noise disturbing the peace every weekend and all those people parking wherever they want. It's as bad as those inconsiderate 15th and 15th businesses. I hope they all go broke so I can have some peace and quiet. We should sue every one of them for being a nuisance."

"Now, honey, remember when you talked to the city attorney? He said they have permits and licenses to operate their restaurants and shops. You do like the gelato place. And sometimes they have your favorite licorice flavor. Arguing with the city upsets you and doesn't accomplish anything."

"Gosh darn it! Everyone wants to live in our neighborhood. They drive up our property taxes and clog up my street. Why can't the neighborhood be like it was in the old days? Quiet, neighborly, and no loud music. I hate this modern shiznit."

"I know, honey. Don't you want to sit and watch Lawrence

Welk with me?"

"Son of a bishop, how does Carolyn get away with making all that awful racket? Did you text her like I asked?"

"Yes, I texted her to ask her to turn it down."

"Why don't you go tell her we've had enough? Take your phone and get some pictures."

"Okay, don't get your longies in a twist. I'll walk down to Carolyn's to see what is going on."

[Mrs. Barker returns]

"Well?"

"They do seem a little loud, and people are spilling over onto the neighbor's driveway. And they are charging a twenty-dollar donation. I did take some pictures. Here, take a look."

"Cheese n' Crackers! That's a lot of people. I'm calling the city to complain."

"Remember to be nice, honey. Last time, you lost your temper and said some not-so-nice things. Maybe this time you will find someone who takes you seriously."

[the following Monday morning]

"Hello, Salt Lake City Corporation. How may I direct your call?"

"I want to talk with someone about my neighbor holding loud rock concerts in her backyard every weekend and clogging up my street."

"Sounds like an enforcement issue. I'll put you through."

"Ordinance enforcement. How may I help you?"

"Yes, this is Mr. Barker, and I want to report that one of my neighbors is having loud rock concerts for profit in her backyard every Saturday night. I am tired of the noise and the people, the mess they make, clogging up my street, and all my neighbors feel this way."

"Yes, Mr. Barker. I see you have filed several complaints about the businesses at 15th and 15th. Is your new complaint related to those businesses?"

"No, this is a lady down the street."

"Would this be related to your complaints about Carolyn's Potluck Gatherings?"

"Yes, it is."

"Sir, the city police have visited this property several times to follow up on your complaints. They found no violation of the noise ordinances, unruly behavior, or other issues. However, they did report that the food was great, especially the ribs, chicken wings, and meatballs."

"Well, now she is having loud rock concerts with hundreds of people making a mess, clogging up my street, and charging twenty dollars per person. That can't be legal."

"Would you like to file a formal complaint, Mr. Barker?"

"Jiminy Christmas. Fetch yes, I want to file a frigg'n complaint."

"Sir, there's no need for that kind of language."

"Sorry. I am so sick of all the noise and those idiots parking wherever they want, and no one in the city cares or does anything about it."

"There is a form on our website that you can fill out to file the complaint. Do you have internet access?"

"Of course I do. And golly gee whiz, I can even program my VCR by myself."

"Well, have a nice day, sir, and enjoy the 70s."

"Honey, are you going file a complaint?"

"Good golly gosh, yes."

"What about our neighbors that seem to enjoy Carolyn's gatherings?"

"I don't care. I just want people to stop blocking my driveway."

[a couple of days later]

"Honey, come see this. There is a reporter on TV interviewing Carolyn about her gatherings."

"Why?"

"Apparently, the city has decided that she is in violation of city ordinances, and they will fine her if she continues. Some of the neighbors are being interviewed. They don't seem very happy."

"Good. Maybe now we will have some peace and quiet. I saw the parking enforcement guy giving someone a ticket yesterday. Complaining does work."

[a day later]

"Honey, come here. Another reporter is interviewing Carolyn on the news."

"So what? They can't reverse their decision once the city has ruled that ordinances have been violated."

[a couple of days later]

"Honey, come listen to the radio. Carolyn and a city official are being interviewed."

"Good, the city guy will make it clear that she can't have rock concerts in my neighborhood and flaunt city ordinances."

"The city guy sounds like he is in favor of community events and that the city will allow Carolyn to have gatherings with some restrictions."

"Son of a biscuit. They can't change their minds. That's just Fricker Frack."

[a day later]

"Honey, the parking enforcement guy is looking at your truck and is starting to write a ticket."

"Hey, stop that. You can't give me a ticket. This is my driveway."

"Sir, your truck is blocking the sidewalk, which violates city ordinances. We have had a lot of parking complaints about this street, and I am just doing my job! Here is your ticket. Have a nice day."

"Judas Priest. Pack up the pantry, woman; it's time to move."

Mother's Box

Jayrod P. Garrett

Only a few of the children remember being added to the Box. But I relive that terror every morning as I wake up to a cup of chilled strawberry ice cream next to my bed.

My Daddy drank enough whiskey to start a fire in his belly and murmur to himself. He sat on the cold tile floor in a red and black plaid flannel shirt, a light from my pink Miss Molly Muffet table his only illumination.

He stared right at me as he said, "I'm sorry, baby, I have to do this. It's the only way to protect you from her." For the third night in a row, I watched him place the Glock in his mouth again. Across the room, I whispered to myself over and over, "Please don't do it. Please don't do it." Every time he took it out, I breathed a sigh of relief. Watched him wipe his tears. Take a swig of Jack Daniels. And put the gun back in his mouth.

I'd tried to stop him the first night. He'd hit me so hard, it knocked a tooth out of my mouth. "I'm doing this to protect you." I didn't know what he meant by that. But I learned I wouldn't overpower him.

Instead, I waited hours. The kitchen microwave read 1:43 AM, a full hour since he'd fallen asleep. I tiptoed over to him and turned the gun in his right hand. I remembered last night, when he'd caught me pulling the gun from his hands. He's squeezed my wrist so hard I screamed. And he'd cried us both to sleep chanting "I'm sorry" over and over. This time I pushed a button to make it release the magazine and slid it free.

As I stood, I wanted to kiss his mellow brown forehead good-night. I told myself, "Don't get sentimental, Charmaine. We have to save him." I crossed the room, pulled a plastic chair to the door, unlocked the knob, deadbolt, and sliding bolt. But as I pushed the chair back out of the way, it scraped against the floor and Daddy stirred. I could have sworn he looked right at me, but he slumped back over and went to sleep.

I crept out the door, down the stairs, and ran from the apartments underneath the full moon towards the nearby pier. Daddy's warnings rattled through my head on repeat: "Never go out past dark, Charmaine. The Weirds will be drawn to you." I found myself looking back at the hotel to make certain I wasn't followed. My heart pounded in my chest like a string of firecrackers as I thought about how Mother tried to hurt me when she became one of the Weirds.

Momma was a large brown woman with big hair and a bigger smile. Maybe that's why I didn't believe she was hurting me when she pushed her fingernails into my scalp. "Just a give me a little more power, Sweetie. Then I'll protect you from all the bad people forever," Mother said.

I knelt on the pier, overwhelmed with the vision in my head. Tears streaming down my face like the blood from my head had when I heard the bang from Daddy's gun. Mother's body hit the floor and blood covered everything. Her green dress. My hands. And Mother's face. Daddy picked me up and squeezed me to his chest. "Daddy gots you, baby. I won't let the Weirds take you. Even if it's Mommy."

It was several minutes before I could compose myself again. I knew the cost of believing adults now. And I knew Daddy believed himself, but I couldn't let him hurt himself just to keep me safe. Losing one parent was already too much. Looking into the water, I couldn't see my reflection. And that calmed my heart enough, I dropped the magazine in the water.

I scurried back more cautious than before. Wondering if the Weirds saw me. If they knew what I did. What they would do if they caught us. I opened our apartment door and locked it back up, picking up the chair this time to make less noise. Then I walked over to Daddy and picked up his heavy right arm and wrapped it around myself. I looked up at him, and I thought despite his drunken stupor, he smiled at me. I cuddled into his warmth and slept.

I startled in the morning as he shook me. "Where is it? Charmaine, where is the magazine for my gun?"

I shook my head, feigning ignorance.

He slapped me. "God damn it, child. Where did you put it?"

I fell back and shook my head. "I put it in the lake. I'm not going to lose you too."

He growled and stood. He rummaged through drawers in the kitchen, searching for bullets. "How am I supposed to keep Pandora away now? How, Charmaine? I wasn't going to let her use me." My heart dropped as remembered how Daddy's power worked. Amplification. He was trying to prevent the Weirds from using his amplification. My amplification. What had I done?

He checked the chamber and breathed a sigh of relief. "There's one round left." He pulled the gun to his forehead and whispered a prayer to himself. "Oh God, please keep Charmaine safe."

A loud knock at the door made Daddy clutch the gun to his chest and made my heart stop.

Daddy grabbed and dragged me down the hall. "She knows we're here."

I should have told him it was going to be okay. That I loved him. That he was a good Daddy. But I couldn't process anything before I found myself being placed on the fire escape outside his bedroom window. He kissed my forehead. "Shhhh. Be quiet. Daddy will—" he swallowed—"fix this. Everything will be okay. You just have to run." He slammed the window shut before I could respond.

If I had been a smart girl, I would have run, but I felt too much to be smart. I crept back towards the living room to see what would happen.

Daddy opened the door with his gun pointed at the face the person on the other side. A woman with long golden hair, pale luminescent skin, and a white pantsuit greeted him.

"Good morning, Damarae. I trust you slept well last night," she said.

"I slept well enough, Pandora. I've had time to consider your offer."

"Excellent, I expect you and the child will be delighted to joi—"

Daddy shook his head, put the gun in his mouth, and pulled the trigger.

I screamed.

But the gun didn't go off. Pandora, a woman a third his size, lifted the gun out of Daddy's hand as if he was a child. "I'm surprised you thought that would work. I'm not much for people killing themselves to escape me, Damarae. But if you really want death, I'll give it to you."

She fired the gun at Daddy, and an explosion went off in slow motion. I shrieked as fire filled the room. Daddy fell backwards in a flaming heap. My heart burst. His bottle of whiskey on the floor shattered from the concussive force. My Miss Molly Muffet table flared into slag. The blast threw me from the fire escape to the ground. And darkness engulfed me.

I awoke to my shoulders being shaken. "Charmaine. Charmaine." Mother's voice called out to me. I reached out and clung to my Mother as she picked me up. "I'm so glad you are alright, sweetie."

I held her, remembering Mother's scent. The aroma of freshly burned woo— Mother didn't smell like burned wood. Mother didn't like perfume. She thought it tacky. I lifted my head from the shoulder it laid on to see Pandora's face. "Charmaine, don't you recognize me? I'm your Mother, Pandora."

Something inside me said, "No you're not." But to my own surprise, I placed my head back down on her shoulder and smiled. "Thank you for saving me, Mommy."

Pandora walked with me towards a long black car as my brain screamed, This isn't my Mother. This isn't my Mother. This isn't my—

"Mommy, can we get Strawberry ice cream on the way home?"

She smiled at me. "Of course, sweetie. I'll get you ice cream every morning. Anything for you."

"When will Daddy join us?" I couldn't believe myself. I'd seen her kill my Daddy. What was going on here?

"I'm sorry, Sweetie. Daddy had to leave to protect us. But he told me to take care of you forever. Let's get you that ice cream."

What bothers me the most is every morning, against my will, my good judgment, after three years of being here I still pick up the bowl of bloody ice cream and eat it until I'm licking the bowl clean. What's worse is that of all the dozens of children in the Box, I'm the only one given a kindness like this from Mommy. And the only one Mommy ever touches.

Nico Tyme and the Necklace of Cleopatra

Scott Bryan

Nico's fingers cramped as he held tight to the outside of the balcony. His weight pulled him downward, but he forced his tired hands to strain around the thin posts.

He was grateful to have latched on when he fell off the roof. An unfortunate glance below revealed an awning that stuck out from a door on the first floor. He looked ahead through the posts to the inside of Cleopatra's bed chamber.

There lay the prize. One of the famous queen's beautiful necklaces. Adorned with glittering gems and fine gold. In Nico's home era of the twenty-third century, it was found not too far from this location. Its discovery earned an archaeologist some impressive coin.

Despite almost plummeting to the ground, Nico's plan could still work. It was easy enough to steal his father's prototype time travel device. Now he was back during the height of Queen Cleopatra's rule, and the same necklace lay before them, ready for taking.

All they had to do was snatch it, rebury it where he could be the one to uncover it and gain the riches for the profound discovery. His twin sister Justine never would've thought of such a plan.

As for his absentee father, the great Professor Nicolas Oscar Tyme was always too distracted with his inventions, his lectures, and anything else to even notice that his disappointment of a son was off on a treasure hunt through history.

Unfortunately, things had gotten off to a shaky start. Instead of sneaking through the fabled Queen's bedchamber, it was his sometime chaotic assistant inching towards the prize.

Nico's heart remained in his throat as his faithful sidekick, TicToc, silently made his way through the legend's room towards her bed.

He was grateful for the clouds that obstructed the moon. Anything to allow the night's darkness to obscure their activities was welcome. The Queen's personal guards hadn't spotted them... yet.

"Hurry," Nico whispered with more of a painful grunt than he planned. "I'm slipping, and the guards below could turn around at any moment."

All he received was a typical, "Eeek. Eeek," as if to say, "Yeah, shut up. You have the easy part. Quick nagging me."

His sometimes-faithful monkey carefully inched around the various furniture. He lightly stepped towards the small table near Cleopatra's sleeping form. Nico couldn't believe he was just a few feet away from one of history's most famous pharaohs.

TicToc latched onto the Queen's necklace and began to scamper towards him. Elation lit up the monkey's face... until he tripped over a pair of leather sandals decorated with jewels.

As per usual, the little simian performed two routine tasks at that moment. He grabbed up the shoes with the precious gems as he'd been trained to do and screamed in shock (or delight) as he bounded towards Nico.

"Eeek! Eeek!" The brave capuchin monkey squeaked as he bounded too quickly towards Nico, who tried to adjust his grip on the posts.

"No, not so fast. Slow down!" Nico shouted.

Cleopatra sat straight up in her bed. Shock crossed her beautiful eyes, followed by confusion and then fear. She shouted in alarm. Thanks to the translator implant all citizens of Nico's native twenty-third century had, he knew exactly what she said: "Guards! Thief!"

The impact, though small, of TicToc's landing on Nico's shoulder was enough to make him lose his grip. He fell downward, his feet slamming into the awning below. Unfortunately, silk awnings aren't meant to support a boy's weight. It ripped, dropping him into the vegetable stand below.

He fell off the now broken stand and slid down the declined road on top of several loose produce. Onions rolled under the approaching guards' feet, tripping them up. Nico used the opportunity to scramble to his feet and make a mad dash around the royal residence. TicToc threw various cucumbers and radishes at the guards before he scampered behind.

Nico wasted no time stuffing the necklace and sandals in his satchel while he simultaneously searched for a way out. Two javelins struck the wall inches from his back.

If he could just get a moment to set the device, they'd be safe and far from angry men with pointy weapons. His heart practically stopped as the next javelin hit the stone walkway in front of him. He stumbled around it and picked up his pace.

Nico made the mistake of looking back. Angry men dressed in bits of gold aimed javelins at him and shouted for him to halt. With nowhere else to go, he followed TicToc into the open plaza.

If he wasn't running for his life, he'd gawk at the shear majesty of it all. The city of Alexandria was vast. In the distance, he saw a huge temple built to Cleopatra's honor, with two magnificent large sphinxes and tall, mighty columns that marked the entrance to the Queen's domain.

Large steps led down to the water, where various boats sat, tied to the dock. The steps were open and exposed; however, at their top, before the temple, were multiple tents where people slept, with the hope of seeing their queen in the morning.

Nico took a chance and ducked into one. Soft lumps on a mat revealed the owners of the closest tent, deep asleep. A sharp sensation ached from his side and his heavy breathing demanded rest. He reached into his satchel to retrieve his dad's device, relieved he could finally stop for a moment.

TicToc began to fiddle with a bowl still lined with traces of leftover food. Nico gestured to him to stop even as he heard the guards shuffling outside.

The capuchin monkey froze in his spot. His eyes grew wide. He instinctively dropped the bowl, which clattered on the stone ground. It reminded Nico that his life wasn't so easy.

"Over there," a guard shouted. "In the tents."

"Come on." Nico hissed as he threw a blanket over his head and, as quiet as possible, slipped out of one tent into another. Even as he escaped the first, he heard the guards' swords as they cut in the previous tent. The sleeping people shouted in surprise, as did those in the tents he pushed through.

He and TicToc didn't stop to excuse or explain themselves. People complained and screamed at him, but he kept on, desperately trying to find a place to hide for a tiny moment until he could permanently escape this place and time.

Sometimes spears and javelins pierced the tents, other times people tried to grab him. TicToc bit a man on the ankle which caused him to let go of Nico, but his shout of pain was all it took to reveal Nico's whereabouts.

"This isn't working," Nico exclaimed as he pushed into another tent. "We need to… wait."

It was empty. The only occupants were stacks of baskets full of goods. Nico quickly lifted a basket, dumped some of the grain it contained onto the floor, and climbed in with TicToc.

"No time to adjust it," Nico explained as he pulled out his father's prototype Chronal Displacement Device. "I wanted to take us miles away but—"

The basket lid was thrown off. The sneering face of a guard bore down on him. He raised his sword, and Nico had no choice but to press the button.

The familiar twinge in his stomach informed him that time travel was underway. The enclosed space around him gave way, which allowed his arms and legs to relax. He felt the rough floor beneath him which instantly assured him he was free from danger.

Until cannon fire exploded the world around him.

TicToc screamed as he clung onto Nico's neck so hard he almost cut off his air supply. Nico barely noticed as chaos reigned in this new world he found himself in.

People scurried for cover as various men shot through broken windows. Gunpowder filled Nico's nose and explosions rocked his ears. A constant zipping whizzed past his head and once he saw bullet holes appear in walls, furnishings, and screaming people—he knew what the sounds meant.

He wasted no more time as he leapt over furniture and dodged terrified people until he found an over tuned table to hide behind.

"This isn't Egypt! This isn't Egypt!" he repeated over and over as he fiddled with his father's device.

All the while, TicToc screamed in his ear as if to shout, "No $#!# you moron! Get us out of here!"

A rough country voice spoke up, "Now where did you come from?" A thin man with brown hair and a hat made from the fur of a racoon aimed his rifle out a window and fired. He ducked back in just before more bullets ripped through the window.

The man continued to speak to Nico, "Don't just sit there.

Grab a gun and help us!"

"Help you? I don't even know where I am!" Nico shouted back.

The man fired his rifle again and smiled. "I always say, whenever a fellow gets bad lost, the way home is just the way he don't think it is. This rule will hit nine times out of ten."

"Crocket," another man shouted. "They're more around the west side!"

"Crocket? Davy Crocket?" Nico checked. "This is the Alamo? 1836? Stupid machine!"

He slammed his hand down on the device again and once more felt the pull of the timestream. His stomach threatened to give up what little breakfast he'd had. Before he could catch his bearings, he discovered no ground just behind his feet. He fell backwards, down a hard slope.

Nico tumbled downward through scratchy, prickling bushes and against rough rocks. All the while, TicToc screeched and screamed at him from somewhere above. His infuriating companion managed to catch some form of security. Monkeys had all the luck.

After several minutes of agonizing crashes and painful tumbles, he finally came to a raw halt in a thorn bush, with spikes far bigger than he'd seen in his life.

He flinched multiple times as he carefully extracted himself from the monster foliage. Nico dropped to a bleeding, red heap on a dirt mound. He looked up at TicToc, who decided it was the best time to smile back at him while hanging upside down from a vine.

Oppressive heat stuck his clothes to his sore skin. Gone was the cannon fire, the gun fire and the terrible noise of multiple desperate people at the end of their rope.

Still, their terrified voices echoed in his thoughts. Nico was only at the Alamo for a couple minutes, yet the terror in the faces of those people still haunted his mind. He thought of Davy Crocket. While a warm firmness controlled the legend's body, behind those eyes lay certain fear.

Nico shook his head. The pain caused by rolling down a hill full of danger bushes made his entire body throb. Despite the eternal ache, his words flowed out to his simian companion, "No. This isn't what we set out to do. We weren't supposed to see that. I never wanted to go to the Alamo."

He forced his throbbing body to sit up. "It was supposed to be easy. Find out where an expensive ancient artifact was uncovered, 'borrow' dad's prototype, go back and get the item, relocate it miles away, bury it, go back and 'discover' it myself."

"Eeeek! Eeeek!"

"It woulda worked!" Nico shot back. "Dad's always too busy to have noticed. Heck, it could still work!"

"Eeeek! Eeeek! Eeeeeek!"

He pushed himself up on scratched, wobbly legs. "No, look." He fished into his bag and pulled out the necklace of Cleopatra. The sandals fell out to the jungle floor. He held the necklace high. "See? We still have it!"

Nico stuffed it back into the satchel and noticed the glittering gems on the sandals. "You had to do it. Didn't you?"

TicToc continued to bounce and fidget on the vine. "Eeeek! Eeeek! Eeeek! Eeeeeek!"

"No. No. No excuses. We stick to the mission, remember?" He pulled out the Chronal Displacement Device. "I'll just reset this back to Egypt, about twenty miles from our last location should do it."

At first, Nico thought the monkey's incessant chattering and bouncing was the cause of the ground shaking. Then he realized that couldn't be right.

It was the deep, predatorial roar as well as the thunderous thrashing came closer that finally gave him his clue.

It's amazing what the human body can do when faced with the concept of extinction.

Despite forgotten aching muscles and throbbing sinews, Nico Tyme pushed himself as fast as he could. He leaped rocks, tore down trails, and swung on branches, all the while shouting, "Not dino food! Not dino food! Not dino food!"

Behind him, a thundering monster from the Triassic period smashed through the foliage. A twenty-foot Tyrannosaurus Rex barreled down on its afternoon lunch, despite Nico's protests otherwise.

He chanced a glance at the device still clutched in his tightened hand and shouted, "Climb on, buddy!"

Once TicToc gripped onto his shoulder, he slammed the button. The hot jungle gave way to more cannon fire and more rocking under his feet. Thanks to his time travel, he surrendered his breakfast onto a wet wooden floor. He needed to stop flipping through the eras and take a break. His hands began to twitch.

He jumped as more explosions shook the world. Chaos drew his attention everywhere while TicToc screamed in his ear. At first, he thought they were back at the Alamo, until he saw the endless horizon of ocean before them. Men shouted as they savagely fought on the deck of what Nico realized was an old sailing ship.

Swords clanged, wood exploded, and more gunpower sifted in the ocean breeze. Nico and TicToc didn't waste time. He ducked an oncoming sword, dropped, swiped his leg to trip an unsuspecting pirate, and then made for the ship's cabin.

TicToc screamed once more as he hopped from pirate head to pirate head. He stole a hat with a beautiful ruby and followed Nico towards their only sanctuary.

Nico spotted a beautifully majestic ship on the portside, loaded with just as many fighting men. He felt the brush of air as a cannon ball passed his head by a foot. It caused him to let out an involuntary shout as he struck the cabin door.

Forcing it open, he ran smack into an imposing figure on the other side. A commanding presence looked down on Nico and TicToc. Even the monkey cowered from his spot on Nico's chest. He knew exactly who this was and what he'd do with Nico's prize tucked safely within his satchel.

A circle of smoke lightly shrouded a hard, powerful face adorned in a thick long beard as dark as the deepest night. Broad shouldered, the imposing figure towered over the boy and demanded, "And just who the devil are you? A stowaway on the Queen Anne's Revenge?"

"Nope." Despite the increasing aftereffects time travel caused, Nico pressed his father's device once more. "I am not dealing with Blackbeard today."

The dark, candlelit cabin of one of the most famous pirate ships gave way to a busy dining room full of people deeply engaged in conversation. He sat unnoticed on the floor near a back wall, TikToc still on his chest, fiddling with his stolen pirate hat as he tried to extract the ruby.

Nico waited for his vision to clear, his hands to stop shaking, and his stomach to settle a bit. He listened to the many people nearby who remained oblivious to his sudden presence.

The people's attention was drawn out wide windows on either side of the relatively small dining room. The tops of the windows slanted outward, and it seemed to be evening outside.

They spoke German, but once again he could understand due to his translator implant. Conversations mentioned the New Jersey town of Lakehurst below and their excitement to ride this demonstrational flight of this great airship.

Once Nico heard the name, he bolted up to glance at a promotional flyer on one of the tables. He softly swore and then said, "Not the Hindenburg." He spotted the time on his father's device: 7:25 PM, May 6th, 1937 AD.

A muffled explosion threw him forward, which jolted his satchel to the ground. Screaming people fell as they smashed into each other and furniture. His satchel lost in the chaos, Nico and TicToc found themselves part of a mass of flailing, panicked bodies.

Hot, stifling fire consumed the room. People leapt from the windows as the flames began to engulf everything. Nico felt the flames lick his skin as his jacket caught fire. Panic exploded within as self-preservation went into overdrive.

This could be it. He only wanted to make some big bucks, and now they were going to die. On the Hindenburg. Where no one would even know. Not his father. Not his twin sister. Just another of his failures, this time for good.

Nico pushed forward, shutting his thoughts away, and with one arm clutched onto his screaming simian companion and his other hand desperately pressing the Chronal Displacement Device, he leapt for safety to the ground below.

Another lurch as the eras sped by. Nico felt the cold embrace of water hit his face and instantly cool his body. Pain lanced through his right shoulder when he hit the bottom of whatever pool he must've landed in. A bed of glittery coins lined the bottom, suggesting where he was.

He erupted to the surface to discover it wasn't a pool, but the Captain Johnathan Worthenton commendable fountain, located at the center of the California Institute of Technology. The device read: February 16th, 2285 AD. He was home.

Thin whisps of smoke left his charred yet soaked clothes. He climbed out of the fountain and sat on its edge. TikToc collapsed beside him, spent. His satchel along with the sought after Cleopatra's necklace long gone.

Death came way too close this time. Death by Egyptian javelin. Death by gunfire. Death by dinosaur. Death by cannon fire or sword. Death by fire. And for what? So, he could prove to his father or Justine that he was worth something? Would they even notice?

After a few moments spent in silence, ignoring the stares from passing students, Nico sighed and said to his constant companion, "Well, it could've been worse. I suppose I should take something from this. Some lesson. What are we even doing? That was way too close, pal."

"Eeek." TicToc replied as he stared blankly into the distance.

"Yeah. I suppose. I mean, how do we know it would've worked?"

After a few more moments of silence, Nico added, "But the money we could've earned. That would've been nice."

Nico sat straight up. "Wait a minute. What if we relocated the lost Irish Crown Jewels?"

Grin & Co.

Fred Smullin

Olivia walked up Main Street in Park City, glancing through shop windows, hoping to shake the loneliness weighing her down. Her reflection in the glass showed her curly blonde hair pulled back in a loose bun and tired eyes. She tugged her sweater closer, feeling out of place among the stylish window displays. But it was off-season, so who was there to impress?

Lost in thought, she suddenly felt a wiggling touch in her palm. "Aah!" Her arm recoiled into the air, her head turned, and her feet danced involuntarily. She saw a young girl standing beside her with a headband of bunny ears—one straight and one flopped over. The girl, about five or six, wore a white blouse, khaki shorts, and blue Crocs. Her lips quivered as she drew her hand close.

Olivia crouched as she caught her breath, offering a gentle smile. "Oh, honey, I'm sorry! You surprised me."

A woman rushed over, apologizing breathlessly. "She's fast, and we're still working on boundaries."

"It's fine," Olivia said, clutching her chest. "I didn't see her."

The little girl's eyes filled, and she looked down, her bunny ear shaking slightly. Olivia's heart softened, and she knelt further. "It's okay. You made my day."

The girl managed a tiny smile, her gaze lifting.

At that moment, Olivia's dark depression from being divorced, lonely, and childless faded away, if just for a moment. She saw a version of herself young and innocent again.

"Are you going to be a bunny for Halloween?" Olivia asked.

The girl's eyes brightened, and she nodded enthusiastically, the floppy ear bouncing, making Olivia chuckle.

The woman sighed. "Come on, Clarissa. This lady has things to do."

Clarissa's lip jutted out. She looked at Olivia, her voice barely a whisper. "Story."

"Story?" Olivia glanced at the woman, eyebrows raised.

"She wants you to read to her. But don't feel obligated; we've already imposed on your time."

"It's okay, but… I don't have a book to read," Olivia replied with a shrug.

Clarissa pointed beyond them. Olivia turned to see an old, faded sign reading "Grin & Co." She frowned. "How did I miss that store?"

Clarissa dashed to the bookstore window, her bunny ear bobbing as she peered in, her gaze fixed on a children's book with a bunny on the cover.

"Clarissa, no, you have plenty of bunny books at home," the woman scolded.

Olivia joined her, reading the title aloud: "Somebunny Loves You." The cover featured a bunny cuddling a young kit in a meadow.

"Good choice," Olivia smiled. "Would you like me to read it to you?"

"She's imposed enough," the woman replied, though her tone softened when she saw Clarissa's hopeful gaze. "But, if you don't mind… "

Olivia nodded. "She's a delight."

The woman sighed in resignation. "All right. Just behave, Clarissa."

"My name's Olivia," she added, extending a hand.

"Lora," the woman said, smiling tightly. Her posture was neat and reserved. Her dark hair, pulled into a tidy bun, framed her tired yet gentle face.

Olivia knelt beside Clarissa. "Thank you for showing me this bookstore. Should we go inside?"

Clarissa grabbed Olivia's hand and hopped toward the door, her voice a delighted whisper, "Hop, hop, hop."

"Remember to be gentle," Lora called, watching Olivia and Clarissa approach the worn entrance.

As they neared the door, Olivia suddenly felt light-headed, as if the ground beneath her had shifted. The street, so stable moments before, now felt subtly off-kilter. The air around the bookstore was thick, almost pulling her forward. Clarissa tugged on her hand, and Olivia's legs wobbled.

"Careful, Clarissa," Lora warned, her voice tinged with concern.

But the girl's grip tightened, urging Olivia onward. Her fingers brushed the vintage brass doorknob, and a strange pull compelled her to turn it. The door creaked open, releasing a wave of air colder than the fall breeze, smelling faintly of aged paper. Olivia stepped over the threshold without fully realizing it, drawn deeper inside.

The door shut behind them with a soft chime, sealing them in.

As Olivia, Lora, and Clarissa stepped inside the dimly lit bookstore, the towering labyrinth of shelves seemed to stretch on much farther than the small storefront should allow. Shadows danced along the walls, flickering in time with the low, flickering lamps scattered throughout the room. The shop felt like it was from another era forgotten by the rest of Park City's quaint Main Street.

Lora grimaced and braced herself like she was dizzy too. She lifted her hand and put her finger under her nose as she scanned the shop. For a moment, Olivia stood still, regaining her balance and taking it all in. She tried to hide her momentary attack of vertigo from Clarissa and Lora. It had to be vertigo from getting up too fast, she thought.

Then, a soft and smooth voice drifted toward them out of the silence. "Welcome to Grin & Co."

Olivia startled, peered into the room, her eyes landing on a figure lounging lazily behind the counter at the room's far end. The woman stood up with an air of complete calm as though nothing could surprise or unsettle her. She was tall and slender, with sharp, angular features, red hair that was almost orange, and her lips that curled into a slow, knowing smile that never quite reached her eyes.

The woman's gaze slid from Olivia to Clarissa to Lora and then back again as if she were studying them, reading something invisible that hung between them. Her eyes were a strange, shimmering green, shifting as the light hit them. And her smile—it was unsettling, like that of someone who knew far more than she let on.

"I don't suppose you've been here before? No? Well… you've certainly come at the perfect time." She leaned forward slightly, her fingers drumming softly on the old wooden counter.

Olivia swallowed, feeling suddenly self-conscious under the woman's gaze. "No, I haven't," she replied, her voice unsure. "Clarissa saw the 'Somebunny Loves Me' book in the window."

"Ah, yes, a bunny lover, I see. You have a keen eye, young lady. Follow me."

Lora said, "Clarissa, honey, hands in your pockets. Please don't touch anything. Some of these books look very fragile and expensive."

"All stories are fragile, some more than others," the woman

said as she turned the corner. "I'm Serafina."

The woman turned another corner into a little nook of children's stories with a charming love seat, colorful cushions, and pillows that begged to be sat on.

"Ah, here it is," the woman said as she pulled the book from the shelf and handed it to Clarissa.

Olivia said, "Would you like to sit in that lovely seat and read it together?"

Clarissa ran over to the loveseat and took her place, her gaze fixed on the book cover. Olivia sat beside her and held the book with Clarissa. She looked at the cover and read aloud, "Somebunny Loves Me."

"Hop. Hop. Hop," Clarissa said as she leaped out of the chair and hopped past Lora's outstretched arms, who was trying to corral her into the nook.

"Clarissa, honey, come back!" Lora sighed deeply, the sound filled with the kind of weary exasperation only a parent of a particularly stubborn child could muster. Her eyes shot a glance at Olivia as she ran after her. "I told you she was impulsive. Clarrisa, get back here!"

Olivia's eyes welled up as she looked at the woman, her lip starting to pout. Clarissa's light of love and innocence had given Olivia's heart hope. Being rejected at this moment broke that spell. Hope was precious and fleeting. One more case of her life plans being cut short, and it hurt. She wanted to bawl, but not in front of strangers.

Clarissa bounded toward a shelf, grabbing a puzzle box with a triumphant grin. The cover depicted Alice in Wonderland—Alice wide-eyed, the White Rabbit clutching his watch, the Queen of Hearts shouting, and the Cheshire Cat grinning mischievously.

"Clarissa, don't open that," Lora warned, but it was too late.

Clarissa flipped open the lid with one motion, sending puzzle pieces cascading onto the floor. She plopped down, frowning as she tried forcing mismatched pieces together. Frustration crept across her face as the pieces refused to cooperate.

Lora's expression tightened. She knelt beside her daughter, her lips thin, glancing up at Serafina with embarrassment. "I'm so sorry."

Serafina waved it off, smiling warmly. "Don't worry. That's what it's for," she said, her gaze soft on Clarissa.

Lora sighed, exasperation spilling over. "Honestly, dragging people into your whims and wasting Olivia's time like this!"

Olivia flinched at Lora's tone, words cutting into her like barbs, reminding her of childhood moments when her mother's scoldings had caged her spirit. Stop wasting time. Grow up. Everything had to be done right, done efficiently. There was no room for whimsy or mistakes.

Lora's voice grew sharper. "You should be ashamed. Making Olivia cater to your whims! Do you think the world revolves around you? People have better things to do than indulge in nonsense."

Clarissa's shoulders slumped under the weight of her mother's scolding. The words pierced Olivia. She'd once been a childlike Clarissa, curious and full of imagination until her mother's sharp words stifled her joy.

Serafina watched quietly, her knowing gaze flicking between Olivia and Clarissa. She seemed to understand the memories surfacing in Olivia's mind. Her raised eyebrows and pursed lips invited Olivia to confront the wound being reopened.

A surge of anger stirred within Olivia. She couldn't let Clarissa be crushed the way she'd been. She wouldn't live by the old script any longer.

Finally, Olivia spoke, her voice quiet but firm. "Clarissa wasn't wasting my time."

Lora stopped, staring in surprise. "Excuse me?"

Olivia steadied herself, holding her ground. "She's exploring, being curious. That's nothing to be ashamed of. I want to spend time with her."

Lora's gaze narrowed, uncertain for once. Olivia didn't waver, feeling something shift inside her—a piece of her old burden unraveling, thread by thread. Her mother's controlling influence lingered, but it no longer held her captive. Her mother's weight on her shoulders shifted, but it felt lighter. She glanced at Serafina, who stood calmly by, her lips tightened into a thin line, eyes heavy with resignation.

Lora's gaze fell, her eyes welling with unshed tears. She blinked rapidly, trying to contain her emotions.

"I know I can be hard on Clarissa," Lora admitted, her voice thick. "Sometimes, maybe too hard. Clarissa is nonverbal and autistic. It's… it can be so frustrating and lonely. For both of us."

Turning to Lora, Olivia's voice was soft but steady. "I'm sorry if I was harsh earlier. My mother was hard on me, and those memories surfaced when you scolded Clarissa."

Lora sniffed, nodding. "She's so smart. She wants a friend but… the other kids don't understand her. They think she's strange."

As if on cue, Clarissa let out a small coo of delight. She rocked back and forth, her fingers deftly pressing two puzzle pieces together, clicking them into place to complete the White Rabbit. Her face lit up with joy.

The world outside was still distant, but Olivia felt something shift inside her again, a quiet stirring that was more than just survival. Clarissa had stirred something in her chest, something small but unmistakable. She didn't know when it started, but a thread of possibility was rewinding its way into her mind, lifting the fog and reminding her of what it was like to dream and want.

Olivia's heart swelled as she watched her. "Clarissa, you saved me today. In more ways than you'll ever know. I'd love to be your friend."

Lora's breath caught, and she looked up at Olivia, her eyes red-rimmed but hopeful. "Olivia, are you serious? She would love that."

"Maybe Clarissa is helping both of you to see you have more in common than you realize," Serafina interjected, her voice a gentle nudge in their stillness.

Lora glanced at Serafina, then back at Olivia, her vulnerability finally spilling over as tears slid down her cheeks. She reached out, brushing a hand through Clarissa's hair with trembling fingers.

"My mother was stern with me too," she admitted, her voice breaking. "I feel so much pressure to prove I'm a good mother—to her and myself. And I end up putting it all on Clarissa."

Clarissa looked up, her gaze wandering to the window. Without warning, she leaped to her feet, hopping toward a sunbeam streaming through the Grin & Co. window. She twirled, arms out, dust particles swirling like magic as she fluttered her hands like wings.

"What I wouldn't give to live like that again," Olivia whispered, watching Clarissa's joyful movements, her bunny ear flopping with each spin.

Serafina's gaze turned to Olivia, her voice soft and wise. "Every dark corner hides a glimmer of hope. You can be like her again."

Olivia felt a warmth she hadn't realized she'd been missing stir inside her.

Serafina grinned widely at Clarissa, Lora, and Olivia. "Remember when life felt like innocent laughter and fun?"

Lora and Olivia were caught up in Clarissa's joy and murmured in unison, "Yes, I do."

Serafina's voice softened to a dreamy tone. "When did you lose your way? When did you decide there was no time for play, let your friends drift away, and think amends could wait?"

Lora and Olivia exchanged glances, puzzled by the stranger's questions. The silence grew between them until Serafina leaned forward, fixing her gaze on Lora. "Lora, how about you?"

Lora's eyes widened. "How do you know my name? I never told you."

Serafina's smile deepened. "Oh, I know all about you and your mothers."

Now visibly skeptical, Olivia stood beside Lora, trying to make sense of this mystery. "How could you know us?"

Serafina gestured toward a set of five leather-bound books on the shelf. "Your stories are here. Living stories, which I read often to keep up with how you're doing. I care about you at Grin & Co."

Lora crossed her arms defensively, and Olivia raised an eyebrow. Serafina pulled one of the books from the shelf, flipping through it thoughtfully. She looked at Olivia. "Do you remember the first story you wrote?"

Olivia's hand flew to her mouth. "Yes."

A memory surged forward: her small, stapled booklet filled with her first story. She had poured everything into it, staying up late, weaving a tale of a girl who spoke with animals and journeyed to distant lands.

Serafina's gaze softened. "When your mother shut down your heart on this page, it broke mine too."

The memory sharpened. Olivia could see her mother in the kitchen, wiping her hands and a tired frown on her face. "I don't have time for fairy tales," her mother had said. "Focus on what matters. Schoolwork. Chores. Don't waste time on nonsense."

The spark of joy she'd felt dimmed under the weight of her mother's words. Olivia recalled clutching her story, forcing a tight smile, swallowing the lump of disappointment that thickened in her throat. She'd been carrying that weight of hope lost ever since.

Serafina returned the book to the shelf and pulled another, looking at Lora. "And you, Lora? Do you remember the magical kingdom you built?"

Lora's breath caught. "Yes… but how?"

She was back in that autumn memory: the backyard filled with the earthy scent of fallen leaves, her hands busy creating a kingdom from sticks and stones. She had imagined a queen's castle, a forest for adventurers, and a magical garden. Her mother's disapproving voice had cut through her reverie.

"What is this mess? Why waste time on nonsense?" her mother had said, eyes narrowed in irritation.

"A kingdom? Lora, you're too old for childish daydreaming. You need to focus on real things. Life isn't a game."

Her mother's gaze had hardened. "You must start thinking about the future. You can't keep wasting time on things that don't matter. If you don't take control of your life, no one will. Do you understand?"

Lora remembered nodding, stifling her wonder to meet her mother's expectations. She had spent her life in control, only to find herself helpless in the face of Clarissa's unique needs. Have I ever been in control, she wondered, or has it all been an illusion?

Lora remained silent, her heart pounding, as Serafina returned the book to the shelf. She exchanged a look with Olivia, and then they both eyed the front door. Their hearts pounded in their chests, the weight of Serafina's knowledge pressing down on them, suffocating in its certainty.

"Don't worry," Serafina said, "I'm not going to harm you. I'm here to facilitate healing. I know this seems like madness. Of course, it's madness; it's your inheritance."

Olivia said, "Inheritance? I don't understand. What is healing about reminding us of painful chapters in our lives?"

Serafina softly said, "Your mother's pain is your pain, and they don't want you to carry that burden anymore. They want to make amends."

Lora stiffened immediately, her body rigid as though struck by an invisible force. The calm exterior she had so carefully cultivated faltered. Her heart thudded against her chest, a painful rhythm that made her feel both exposed and defensive. The words"They want to make amends" stirred something hidden, something raw that she had worked so hard to bury beneath layers of control.

Make amends? The very thought of it felt like a knife twisting in her. How could her mother, who had spent years shaping her into something brittle and unyielding, want to make amends? Lora's mind immediately rebelled against the notion. Her mother had never been the type to apologize, to show vulnerability. She had been a towering force who wielded control like a weapon. And yet, here was this stranger—Serafina—suggesting that her mother's harshness had come from her pain.

It felt like a trap. Serafina's words offered something soft and comforting, but accepting them meant acknowledging a truth Lora wasn't ready to face. That her mother's actions, all those years of trying to mold her, had been born from her unspoken wounds. And what would that mean for her? If her mother had suffered, had her pain—what did that make Lora's suffering?

A hot surge of anger bubbled up in her chest, clashing with the unexpected swell of sadness that threatened to break through.

Her nails dug into her palm as she forced herself to remain composed. She wouldn't let anyone, especially a stranger, unravel her like this. Lora's jaw tightened, her lips pressed into a thin line. She couldn't believe it, wouldn't believe it.

Make amends? After all this time? It was too late.

Lora glanced at Olivia and back to Serafina as she said, "Why should we trust you?"

Olivia was still processing Serafina's words. The moment Serafina spoke, a tremor passed through her, subtle at first but enough to make her knees feel weak. Her chest tightened, and her breath came in short, uneven bursts as though someone had opened a door she had long kept sealed. Once buried deep in her memory, her mother's face suddenly rushed forward with startling clarity, flooding her with the familiar weight of her childhood.

"Your mother's pain is your pain…"

Olivia's throat constricted, her vision blurring at the edges. She hadn't thought of it like that before, had never allowed herself to consider that the sharp words, the controlling hand, the constant pressure to be something she wasn't, had come from her mother's wounds. Her mother had been relentless—constantly pushing, always demanding perfection. And Olivia had carried that burden, trying so hard to meet impossible expectations, until the joy she once felt had been smothered under the weight of it all.

But now, Serafina was saying that the pain wasn't all hers. That her mother, the one who had seemed so unmovable, had her grief, her struggles. They wanted to make amends.

Olivia's heart cracked open just a little at those words. The thought was both painful and strangely tender. Her mother had been gone for years. The wounds long scabbed over but not healed. The idea that her mother, somewhere beyond, might regret those years and might want to make things right was almost too much to take in. It made her chest ache, a deep, yearning ache that she had tried to ignore for so long.

Tears pricked at the corners of her eyes, and she blinked them away; thoughts jumbled in her mind, too fast to catch, too sharp to ignore. Every breath felt jagged; each inhale was a struggle against the overwhelming rush of feelings that twisted inside her. She had never expected an apology and had stopped hoping for one long ago. But Serafina's words offered a sliver of something she hadn't realized she needed: the possibility of forgiveness for her mother and herself.

But could she accept that? Could she let go of the resentment she had carried for so many years? Olivia felt something shift inside her, a stirring she hadn't expected. It was fragile, but it was there.

Olivia glanced at Lora, who stood stiff and silent beside her. There was tension between them—two daughters whose mothers' wounds had shaped them, each grappling with the possibility of letting go. Olivia could feel the hesitation, the resistance, but also the faint hope that maybe, just maybe, there was a way forward.

Serafina watched them both, her smile soft, knowing she had seen this unfold many times before.

"You don't have to carry it forever," Serafina said gently, her voice like a distant echo, offering them the choice to hold on or to let go.

The air inside Grin & Co. felt heavier now, as though everything Serafina had said had stirred the weight of years of unspoken words and untended wounds. Lora and Olivia stood side by side, both silent, their hearts still processing the ripple effects of the conversation. The once-oppressive atmosphere in the shop felt different now, quieter but filled with anticipation, as though the moment had been leading to this all along.

Serafina smiled softly, her eyes gleaming with something more than the usual mystery. There was a deep knowing in her gaze—a wisdom that seemed timeless and gentle as if she understood the journeys of both women better than they understood themselves. Without a word, she moved to a shelf and reached into a small, polished wooden box. When she turned back to them, her hands cradled two smooth, white stones, each shaped like a heart, white as the first snowfall.

Her fingers brushed over the stones as though they held the world's weight in their simple forms. She approached Lora and Olivia slowly, her steps measured and each movement deliberate as if she were guiding them through something sacred.

"I've been holding these for you," Serafina said, her voice barely above a whisper, as though she were sharing a secret. She held out the stones, one in each hand. They glistened faintly in the dim light.

Serafina smiled, her eyes twinkling with that familiar, knowing glint. "These stones," she said softly, "are not just stones. They are your hearts. They remind you to tend to them, plant something new in them, forgive, love, and heal. The past doesn't define you anymore. You are free to write your own story. And whatever you choose… let it be what your heart truly wants."

Lora and Olivia exchanged glances, each sensing the unspoken significance yet still caught in the quiet power of the moment. Lora's hand trembled as she reached for the stone, her fingers brushing against its cool surface. She hesitated, feeling something stir in her chest—something that had been buried for so long; it was unfamiliar now.

Serafina placed the stone gently in her hand. "This," she said softly, looking into Lora's eyes, "is not a burden. It's a gift. A reminder that your story is not written in stone—it still has blank pages to fill. You've carried your mother's pain for so long, thinking it was yours to bear. But it isn't. It never was. Now you can begin again."

Lora swallowed hard, her throat tight, but something inside her softened. The cold hardness she had lived with for so many years—her armor, her shield—began to crack just a little. The stone in her palm felt light and warm now as if absorbing the heat of her hand. She nodded, though her words failed her, and for the first time in what felt like forever, she allowed herself to believe that there could be more to her story.

Serafina turned to Olivia next, her gaze as tender as it was unwavering. "And for you, Olivia," she said, placing the second heart-shaped stone into Olivia's open palm. "You've spent so long trying to perfect your script, following lines that weren't yours to follow. But now... now you can write whatever your heart leads you to write. You have permission to let go of the expectations, to find joy in the blank page again."

Olivia's chest tightened as she looked down at the stone, the smoothness of it comforting in a way she hadn't expected. A tear slipped down her cheek, unbidden, but she didn't wipe it away. Serafina's words reached a place deep inside her, a place she had hidden from herself—her need for control, her fear of failure, her longing to feel free again.

Her heart ached, but not in the way it used to. It was the ache of something new—of possibility, of healing. As she held the stone, she felt the weight of her mother's expectations, her fears, and the script she had been following for so long begin to lift.

There was silence between the three of them—Lora, Olivia, and Serafina—as if the air around them understood the moment's significance. Clarrisa broke the silence, uttering intensifying squeals as she flapped her arms and tilted her head. She stood fixated on the dust particles that danced like miniature fairies in the sunbeam.

"How can any of this be real? I must be dreaming," Lora whispered.

Lora and Olivia stood there, holding their stones. Their hearts quietly shifted, and their stories opened up before them.

Serafina stepped back, her smile softening into something more divine. "It's time," she said, though the words were gentle, almost a release. "My work here is done. Take your gifts and bless the world outside that is waiting for you to live your stories."

Olivia blinked, suddenly aware of how much lighter she felt. She glanced at Lora, who nodded, her resolve quietly shifting. The beam of light that had captivated Clarissa vanished. Clarissa took their outstretched hands, and they turned toward the door. The heart-shaped stones were still warm.

Lora and Olivia were filled with questions, still reeling from what they'd experienced, but a gentle force seemed to push them toward the door. The doorbell chimed softly as they stepped outside. The world around them shifted again, tilting just enough to make them stumble like the ground was rearranging itself.

Main Street's cool autumn air brushed against their faces. They stood in the sunlight, taking in a world that felt warmer and more alive. Olivia noticed tears glistening on Lora's cheeks as she knelt beside Clarissa, hugging and stroking her hair.

Olivia wiped her eyes, her heart feeling lighter. For the first time, her struggles seemed understood, named aloud, and somehow powerless. She turned back to see Grin & Co., eager to take one last look at the place that had transformed her and say thank you to Seraphina. But when she did, she gasped.

Lora heard her and turned, her eyes widening. The bookstore was gone. All that remained was a blank wall of weathered bricks, as if Grin & Co. had never existed.

Clarissa was the first to notice a book lying against the wall.

She ran to her "Somebunny Loves Me" book and clutched it in her hands.

Olivia leaned down, whispering to Clarrisa, "Somebunny does love you."

"Lora, did you... see that coming?" Olivia whispered, half-laughing in disbelief.

Lora let out a breathless chuckle. "Not even remotely. Did our mothers lure us into a therapy session?"

"It's just my luck that the strangest yet best therapy session I've experienced has disappeared."

They exchanged a nervous laugh, the tension between them lightening. Lora glanced down at Clarissa, whose bunny ears flopped as she surveyed Main Street, still holding her book.

Olivia said, "Coffee? I think we deserve something warm and comforting."

Lora nodded, her face softening. "Absolutely. There's a lot we need to unpack."

Clarrisa had led Olivia to the best possible gifts: meaning and purpose. The overwhelming weight of rejection and depression was gone. Olivia's heart felt light as a feather. A blank page lay before her, and she silently vowed to write a story with Lora and Clarissa as long as they would allow. Olivia's pain would not be Clarissa's. She'd have a better childhood than they had experienced.

Olivia looked down at Clarissa with a smile. "And what about you, my new friend? How about a treat?"

Clarissa's eyes brightened, and she gave a big nod. "Cookie," she said, the floppy ear bobbing in agreement.

Olivia said, "I'm happy we are in the middle of a new chapter."

Lora smiled, her own heart lighter. "Let's make it a good one for Clarissa."

 Princess

Talysa Sainz

It's Beauty and the Beast,
she told herself.
She loved his every perfection,
his softly golden hair
and blue velvet eyes,
the way his lips curved
when he was happy.
He knew how to charm everyone
into falling in love with him.
She was no exception--
but her flaws were too much to ignore.

Maybe it's Cinderella, she thought.
His wealth of positive attributes
in stark opposition to her lack.
She talked too much, oversharing,
constantly worrying
about pleasing everyone.
Desperate, he called her. Annoying.
It's better than I deserve, she reasoned,
when he broke his promises
or insulted her.

Perhaps it's Sleeping Beauty.
After all, he had surely rescued her
from a living death.

But she wondered each day
if he would ever love her
enough to light up his face.
If he would smile for her
as if he still needed to win her over.
If he would appreciate
her sacrifices to be loyal to him
amidst his indiscretions.

It's Snow White, she concluded.
She had taken that fateful
bite of the poisoned apple.
The man she had fallen for
turned out to be nothing more
than the villain who poisoned her.
She didn't see the darkness lurking
behind his ever-charming face
or the monstrous urges
that would eventually take over
his playful persona.

Maybe she didn't want to be
a princess anymore.
No crown was worth this.
She found more love
from the woodland creatures,
the mice, the enchanted furniture,
than she did from her supposed Prince.
She couldn't wait for someone
to love her back to life.
No, in the end,
she could only rescue herself.

The Third Man

Johnny Worthen

The plane fell and rose at the mercy of the weather. Oliver thought it a fit metaphor for his life of late. Plummet, recover, hear assurances before another fall. Loss and recovery, loss and recovery, always powerless to change anything. A storm since Cheri's death, the loss of a lighthouse that now showed the inadequacies of his own life in stark collapsing detail.

"Cheri was her own girl," said Marshall over the headset.

"What? Oh, yeah. You dated her once in high school, didn't you?"

Marshall just nodded. His attention was on the controls. He was the pilot of this new plane. No, Oliver remembered, he was the owner of this new plane. How far his friend had come since college. They were once so close, but now had hardly seen each other in years.

It was a new plane, but it was a little plane – a four-seater, top wing, wheels permanently hanging below the fuselage. Headphones required. The din of the engine so near and the perils of the altitude so close outside that they had to be muffled if one expected to function within. Another metaphor?

"When did we last hang out?" Oliver said into the microphone. "You and me?"

"I think it was at Scott's wedding last year."

"That was the last time we saw each other, but we didn't hang out then."

"No, we didn't," said Marshall. "I guess it was sometime be-

80

fore that."

Oliver had gone on to graduate school, Marshall into business. Marshall always was a mover and shaker, the one who had the connections and could network a cemetery, as he used to say. Cemetery.

"What made you reach out?" said Oliver.

"I wanted to see you again. I—"

A gust jarred the plane up suddenly.

"Should we be flying in this?" asked Oliver.

They were somewhere between St. George, Utah and Denver, Colorado, over snow-peaked mountains that were closer than Oliver felt was appropriate. The weather front was foreseen but Marshall had assured him he'd flown through worse.

"I've flown through worse," he said.

"Where?"

"A hurricane off Cozumel."

"Mexico?"

"Last time I checked."

The plane rose and leveled. Out the window the purple mountains vanished behind a cloud that wetted the window.

"We could have just hung out in St. George," said Oliver.

"Yeah, but I have a pool."

"I have a pool."

"I meant pools. And a tennis court."

"What? When did you learn to play tennis?"

"I don't play. It came with the house. I wanted something near the slopes."

"Why not Salt Lake?"

"My business was based in Denver."

"Vale isn't Denver."

"Yeah, but Denver has issues. I'd like to be in Aspen, but it's too hard of a commute from there."

"I don't understand. Wha's your job?"

"I'm retired now. Done."

"When did you retire?" Oliver examined his old friend. They were the same age, thirty-three. Retirement was a dream Oliver hadn't even considered yet and yet Marshall had achieved it. He felt like he'd missed not just the train, but the station.

"I retired the day I heard about Cheri," Marshall said.

That sat strange.

"No offense, dude," said Oliver, "but you didn't even come to the funeral."

"I couldn't make it. I sent flowers."

"Did you?"

"I was told they arrived. I'll be pissed if they didn't come."

"I don't remember. It was a shit day. I wasn't looking at the flowers. You could have called."

"And said what?"

Oliver had to shake his head at that. "Yeah, okay."

"Truth be told, Ollie, I'm a chicken shit. I couldn't come to the funeral because I was a chicken shit."

"Your date didn't end well? I don't think I want to hear this."

"What did Cheri tell you? About herself? At the end?" Marshall tapped on a dial and swore under his breath.

"She said nothing," said Oliver. "Like you, we'd lost touch. I only heard about it because our names matched in her phone. I got a call from the police during a meeting."

"Who found her?"

"A neighbor complaining about her dog crying. It'd been crying for days."

"What happened to the dog?"

"A friend took it."

"You didn't know she was using?" asked Marshall.

"No, of course not," said Oliver. "I... No..." He sighed.

"Maybe. We all have our own issues."

"You still seeing Marie?"

"No. She left me for a gauge-wearing barista."

"How'd that work out?"

"He left her for a bigger breasted barista."

"And the world turns. You dating anyone now?" asked Marshall.

"Not really. A girl from work might be interested, but I'm afraid to ask her in case it's some kind of HR trap."

"Ick."

"You still haven't explained your reappearance in my life," said Oliver.

"Don't you need a vacation?"

"I do," he said, "but this has kind of a kidnapping feeling to it."

"It is a kidnapping."

"You didn't say that with enough humor."

"Wait, you don't actually feel scared, do you?"

"No." And it was the truth. Marshall had called Oliver out of the blue, told him to clear his calendar for the weekend, and meet him at the airport Friday afternoon. Marshall knew where he lived, a detail about the other Oliver could not reciprocate Old friendships, though, are enduring and eternal. Even after years of separation, they'd fallen into the same vibe as they'd had in grade school, middle school, high school, college dorm. He knew Marshall.

"Cheri was a good person," said Marshall.

"They arrested her two usual dealers on murder charges, but it didn't stick. She got the drugs somewhere else. She had a third dealer somewhere."

"I gave her the drugs," said Marshall.

"Not funny."

"No. It's not."

Oliver turned to stare at his friend in the dim light. Outside and around dark threatening clouds thickened.

"I gave it up the day I heard she OD'd," said Marshall. "I flew the shit in from Mexico to the US."

"You're a smuggler? That's your job?"

"Was."

"You're a goddamn murdering drug dealer?"

"Was."

"You're serious? This is really pissing me off. She was my fucking sister, my family. Your fucking family. Tell me this is a terrible fucking joke."

The plane bucked and shifted. The engine coughed once but returned to its droning. Marshall scrutinized his panels before turning the cockpit heater up to maximum.

"I quit that life," he said. "I was a user too. Every bit as bad as Cheri for a while. I knew what she was going through. So… Well… I'm doing the steps now, Ollie. You're my ugly number nine. I need to confess and make amends. I didn't know she was going to die. It wasn't a hot dose. She might have—"

The engine coughed, sputtered, and stopped.

Marshall threw switches, pulled levers, steered the plane.

"What's going on?" said Oliver.

"Engine's out."

Oliver dared take his headset off and heard only the wind against the fuselage. His vision was obscured for the clouds, but he could clearly see the unmoving propeller at the nose of the quiet plane.

"Mayday mayday mayday. Stationaire 6-5-2 Alpha Tango declaring emergency. Engine failure. Bearing East north east out of Grand Junction. Losing altitude. Bad weather."

The wind pushed and twisted the falling plane in risings and fallings, terrible fallings. A silent rollercoaster.

Oliver said, "What should I do?"

"Buckle up," said Marshall.

"What?"

"We're going to—"

Shattering plastic, breaking glass, twisting metal. Silence become a scream of splintering wood and ripping wings. Crash. Pause. Shift. Fall, and crash again.

It took Oliver a moment of waking to realize he was upside down. It took him a couple more moments to remember where he was and what had happened. It took him a terrible few more moments to realize he couldn't see. He touched his face and felt pain, felt glass, warm blood, but freezing in the paralyzing cold that was all around him. Pain.

He felt around and met jagged edges and poking sticks. Above him, really below, a snowy ground. Fumbling for his belt, he managed to collect his courage enough to open the clasp and tumble down.

More pain. A bruised shoulder to add to the list. He sat up and took inventory. His shoulder now, his eyes darkened, his face a scab of blood, but nothing broken or gushing he could feel. But there was cold.

"Hello," he said and received no reply. "Marshall!" He yelled again, but it was as if his words were absorbed into the world around him. No answer, no echo. He imagined deep snow, thick flakes falling. The silence of such scenes had always haunted him for their beauty. The muffling of a white world as it was draped in tender snow.

"Marshall!" he tried again.

He was cold. Getting colder. They had crashed somewhere in the Colorado Rockies, famous for their ruggedness.

"Marshall?" a question this time. "Are you there?"

"Time to move, Oliver," said Marshall. "Our SOS wasn't picked up."

"How?"

"We were below the mountains."

"Are you certain no one heard us?"

"Yes. Time to move. Can you move?"

"I'm blind. I can't see."

"Yes, I know. I can't help you."

"Why, what happened to you?"

"You don't want to know. I'm a mess. Can you stand?"

Oliver gingerly got to his feet. He was suddenly aware of how much vision aided in that everyday act. It was alarmingly difficult to stand. He stumped and fell the first two times, the last one on a piece of wreckage that cut into his forearm deep enough to draw blood.

"Shouldn't we just hunker down and wait for help?"

"No. I told you the message didn't get out."

"Then when we're overdue they'll look for us."

"They might, but I didn't file a flight plan."

"What? How? Why not? I thought that was required."

"Habit. I filed a shit one."

"Drug dealing was quite a career choice."

"I'm sorry," he said. "Walk forward."

"Which way is forward?"

"In front of you, smart ass. Head downslope. There's a stream down there and a house a ways off."

"How far off?"

"A ways."

"You don't sound confident we can reach it."

"Get moving. Get warm. Your feet are already freezing."

Oliver stepped forward, tripped, and fell to his knees. The

snow wasn't too deep, only up to his elbows. He'd have preferred to crawl rather than walk but his bare hands couldn't handle it. He crawled a few yards anyway before standing up and tucking his hands under his armpits.

"Keep moving," said Marshall.

"Help me."

"There's a tree to your left. Find a stick under it."

"Your hands are hurt, aren't they?"

"You could say that."

"Bad?"

"Stick. Pick up a goddamn stick, you waste of space, and get moving downslope. The storm will only get worse. If it hits before… Just get moving, you dorkus erectus."

It was an old taunt from fourth grade and had someone survived to be a personal joke between them.

Oliver staggered to the tree, felt the pine bough on his face first, and flinched from the pain of it as it poked his wounds.

"Are my eyes…"

"I don't know. Not important. Get a stick."

He felt around under the tree, pine by the smell, and found a frozen sappy branch that would work as sensing stick. He snapped off the twigs as best he could and then crawled out from under the canopy.

He was alarmed to notice he couldn't feel his feet.

"We should build a fire."

"Downslope. Go."

"Fire."

"You got matches?"

"No."

"I don't know how long I can last, you moron. Get moving downslope."

"What?"

"Stop arguing and start walking."

"You're an asshole."

"I know."

Oliver slowly plowed into the snow. He remembered he was wearing long jeans and a flannel shirt. He was dressed for a southern Utah Spring not a high Colorado blizzard.

He moved steadily for a long time. He listened for Marshall behind him, but didn't hear much over the muffling snow that absorbed sound like water took snowflakes, but Oliver knew he was there.

After a mile, maybe two, an hour at least, his feet were cold, but he could feel them. Thank god he'd worn his hiking boots.

"So this whole trip was to lock me into a room where I literally couldn't escape and hear you confess about killing my sister?"

"Something like that."

"Fuck you."

"Yeah."

"It's not just Cheri, you know. Thousands – hundreds of thousands of people overdosed just last year. You had a part of that."

"I know."

"You know?"

"I'm trying to make amends."

"How could you have done it to begin with? I thought I knew you, man."

"Legalize adulthood," said Marshall. "Remember when I used to say that?"

"Yeah, as an excuse to smoke pot in the park."

"I meant it. I believed it. People should be allowed to do what they want."

"Even OD?"

"I thought so once."

"What changed your mind?"

"Duh."

"Cheri?"

"I loved her."

Oliver held up and turned to face where he thought Marshall was standing. "I don't want to hear this shit. Not from you."

"I broke it off with her."

"No, you didn't. I was there. She left you for Malcolm Allred, all state basketball."

"That was high school. We got together again a few years ago."

"Dream on."

"Her use was out of control."

"You dumped her because she was using? You were using."

"Yes, but she was getting reckless."

"When was all this?"

"A couple years ago. I was just starting out… smuggling… and got cheap supply. I'd done a couple runs from central America and had enough money to be stupid, so I made a move for the girl who was my first crush. She reciprocated. We partied. We got along. Eternal happiness in view."

"Why didn't I know any of this?"

"Because if it got weird, we didn't want you hating on us. Neither one of us wanted the drug thing talked about, and that was honestly a lot of what was happening. We agreed that we'd be friends even if things went bad. We kept that promise."

"With friends like you…"

"Cocaine was my drug of choice. She went harder. We fought eventually and realized we weren't good for each other. And…"

"And?"

"And she was your sister. I didn't want to enable her."

"Listen to yourself. You didn't want to enable her while you're smuggling fentanyl into the country?"

"I didn't get to pick the cargo."

"You're acting like you didn't have a choice."

"It was a dangerous business. Saying no was not always on the table. Hey, steer to the right, there's a big rock there."

"How'd you get out then? Or did you?"

"I went into treatment, told them I was out. They threatened me, I told them, 'That's nice. Have a nice day.' Tree."

"What?"

"You're walking into a tree."

Oliver slammed into a chest-high branch that knocked him on his ass. Worse, it shook the tree which dropped a heavy mass of wet snow directly on him. The cold actually felt good on Oliver's face, soothing the stinging pain around his eyes in a blanket of cool, but it was short-lived. The snow was thick and suffocating and had found its way under his shirt to melt against his now wet skin.

"Get up," said Marshall. Oliver was surprised he could hear him so well half buried as he was, but realized it was a very good idea. He rolled over and got to his knees, his hands again stinging for the elbow-deep snow.

"Up."

Oliver stood up. "I'm tired. It's cold."

"It'll get colder. It's nighttime."

"Is it? I can't tell. How long have we been walking?"

"A few hours."

"Let's rest."

"No. Stopping is death. No one is coming. There's no shelter here. Move."

"Where?"

"The house. There is only one way down but there are cliffs now. You need to move right. Go slow. There's a path along the edge. I'll guide you."

Oliver still had his stick but it did little good as he found himself on what he imaged to be a narrow ledge over an infinite abyss. Side stepping, blind, inch by inch, he moved laterally for an hour, the wind burning his ears until they just stopped hurting.

"I'm losing it," he said.

"A hundred yards more and you can rest."

He made the hundred yards and Marshall directed him behind a fallen tree to catch his breath. "Just for a minute or two."

"I'm dying here," said Oliver.

"You must keep moving, shit head."

"You killed Cheri."

"I couldn't save her."

"You gave her the drugs. Or did you sell them to her?"

"Get up."

Oliver struggled to his feet, leaned on the stick until it bowed, threatening to snap. But it held, so Oliver stood and then walked on.

"You think just because you're in rehab I'll forgive you?"

"I'm doing what I can."

"Cheap excuse."

"Keep walking. The storms getting worse."

And on he walked. The wind was chill and steady, but eerily broken every third or fourth step as he assumed they passed trees or other obstacles to cut the cutting wind.

"Did you get out?" asked Oliver.

"What do you mean?"

"Did these dangerous people you deal with sabotage the plane?"

"I wondered that too," said Marshall, "but it was carburetor icing. It happens. It was an accident."

"You're sure?"

"Yeah."

"But they could still come after you."

"Nah. Looks like we're coming up to a big meadow. Afterwards there's a good canopy of trees. It'll make for slow going, but the wind and snow will be less."

"How much farther?"

"Dawn. Maybe."

"How long is that?"

"Hours."

"What time is it exactly?"

"It's dark."

By the blast of cold and ice, Oliver knew he'd entered the meadow. He could sense the openness somehow, knew the trees were distant, but felt the empty expanse around him broken only by Marshall's presence. He wondered for a moment what his friend's—if he could still call him that—what his friend's injuries were. Something terrible no doubt. And yet, he'd not complained while that was all Oliver had done.

The cold cut him, the silence oppressed him. Somewhere in that meadow, after walking for so long—hours and hours it felt like—Oliver wanted to give up. He slowed, leaned on the stick, and noticed his hands were not functioning right, not releasing their grips, not feeding him their usual information.

"Don't sit. Keep going," said Marshall. "You can do this. I'll see you through. Please, Oliver, I know it's hard, but you have to keep going."

"My life's shit, Marshall. My job sucks. My love life is non-existent. I'm a failure to my family. To myself. I let Cheri die. I let you... I let Cheri die. If I'd have been there... No one will miss me."

"Oliver, when Cheri died, I was heartbroken, but not for her. I knew it would hurt you — not only for Cheri, but for my part in it. It wasn't about you. There was nothing you could have done that would have prevented anything. I suspected it then. I know it now. It was her call. It's taken me years to face this. To face you. I've done some shit stuff, Oliver, I know. I've wronged you, but know that I'm telling the truth now. You're not nothing. You're a good soul and you will get off this mountain and you will know joy again."

"Marshall, where did you go?"

"I went astray, my friend. I forgot to be good like you."

"I'm not that good. I'm a coward."

"You're the nice guy who finishes last. That girl at work wants to know you better. It's not a trap. She's nice. You'll like her. If you try. If you get off this mountain, your life can be bright. Oliver, this is the time. This is the moment of truth. This is where you become the hero like we used to play, when against the odds, we stand at the bridge, brave the storm, and sail on, because you are the hero. This is it, Oliver. You die here if you stop. If you touch the ground here, you will not get up again. No. Hell no. Get your sorry checker-cheating ass up and moving before I mash you!"

It was another reference to their childhood, their golden days together. Oliver had thought at times that they had raised each other. Their parents were hands-off to the level of neglect by modern standards. No helicopter parents were they. Addictions and drugs played a part in both their families. Oliver's dad drank himself to death. Marshall never had one to begin with. Both their mothers were addicted to chemicals and bad social media. Marshall and Cheri followed the family path. Oliver had been the odd man out. In college, he'd tried to be an alcoholic, but failed. Maybe because of his dad's great example. For him, it was always two beers and on to water. Marshall had drank enough for both of them, but somehow it hadn't stopped him.

"You're a success," said Oliver. "Planes and a mansion. Chicks?"

"Things are empty. I never married. Never had anyone I cared enough about to even marry."

"Except Cheri?"

"Except Cheri. Get moving dick-weed."

"You have money."

"I had money."

"Blood money."

"Without a doubt. It's only half a football field to the tree line. It'll be better there. Walk."

"We all die soon or late…"

The wind relaxed as if his words had triggered the change and allowed the snow to come. It fell, thick and heavy and slow, so much so that Oliver, through his pain, felt its landings. What little sound remained was blotted away by the curtain of invisible flakes airborne and carpeting like a killing quilt.

Close to his ear, Marshall whispered, "Oliver, I am limited. I can't carry you. You have to walk. Just take one step. One step, for me."

No step.

"For Cheri."

A step.

"Another for Cheri."

No step.

"Oliver, move for yourself."

No step.

"Then for us, for all of us. For the sunshine and the light and the hope that waits for you away from this frozen mountain. For the dreams we had as children, for the good times that were and will be again. Goddamn it, Oliver! Step! Step!"

A step.

"Step!"

Another. And another, and so it went until Oliver felt with his stick found the trunk of a tree and he was off the meadow and somewhat out of the storm.

Soon warmth returned to Oliver's limbs, and though his extremities were silent with freezing numbness, he knew he made progress and moved on.

"Hey, Marshall, you still there?"

"Always."

He didn't know what do with that. "Isn't there something about the eighth step of AA about not pissing people off?"

"It's the ninth step. 'I will make direct amends to such people wherever possible, except when to do so would injure them or others.'"

"Yeah, that one," said Oliver. "I think you might have crossed the injury line here."

"No doubt," he chuckled.

"You were always getting us into trouble." Oliver felt the cold creeping up into his groin, rising with doom. His legs were rebelling. He was tired beyond measure. He knew his time was nearly done. Regardless of his will, his body would soon fail him.

"Yeah, but I always got us out," said Marshall.

A few more steps. A dozen, then eight. Then three. Then Oliver stumbled and swayed. The cold was so hard.

"I missed you," said Oliver.

"I missed you too, brother."

"I miss Cheri."

"Yeah."

"But you know, I...uhm..." He paused. Stepped, stumbled forward. It was so hard to balance.

"Yeah," said Marshall. "I love you too."

The world spun as the ground rushed up to meet Oliver's

shivering body. A mat of deep snow collected him into its shroud of softness, caressing him in a final wintry embrace he could not resist.

It took him a moment to realize he was still alive. It took him another moment to realize he wasn't freezing and wasn't in pain. In fact, he felt great. It took him another hopeful moment to notice the sounds of a hospital around him and recognize the feeling of painkillers softening the edges of everything.

"Hello," he tried to say, but the word was all growl and rasp. He swallowed, cleared his throat and tried again. "Hello? Hello, anyone there?"

"You're awake," came a kind female voice.

"Wha...?" It hurt to talk.

"You had a tube down your throat for a while, dear. Hold on. I'll get the doctor."

He laid back and recalled the harrowing trek off the mountain and wondered if he'd ever forgive Marshall. Time enough for that later, he decided and fell back asleep.

He awoke, aware that he was in a hospital. He could see it. It wasn't clear, but he saw. He blinked and his vision cleared a little.

A face bent over and examined him.

"I'm doctor Azir," he said.

"My eyes?"

"Your left one was hurt, but it should heal."

"Left?" he realized only his right was open.

"It had glass in it. We removed it. The right was just blood-clotted shut from a cut on your scalp. We cleaned it up. A little corneal damage too, but that'll heal. Your feet and fingers have some frostbite. I don't know when your last pain meds were. Are you in pain? Do you want the patch back on?"

"Yes. No. Maybe."

The doctor appeared to nod in understanding and slid a cool bandage back over his face. The world was again dark, but not so much.

"Doctor?"

"Yes."

"How did I get here?"

"Ha, you fell flat on your face into a snowbank six feet in front of Doris Hamblett's kitchen window while she was making breakfast. Mr. Hamblett is an EMT. They have the only house within miles of where you crashed. Unbelievable you found it. You've been here in the hospital for about three days."

"My friend? Marshall. Is he okay?"

"He was the other man in the crash?"

"Yes."

"I'm sorry, son. He didn't make it."

The news stunned him. For a long moment the information settled like a weight. Guilt and responsibility. Forgiveness? For a dead man whom he'd loved and hated? What steps would he need now to deal with the feelings churning in his mind? Were they numbered? Were they the same as Marshall's?

He was about to ask about Marshall's injuries or, horribly, if the Hamblett's had just not seen him in time, when the Doctor laid a reassuring hand on Oliver's arm.

"Some good news, though," he said. "Your friend's body was recovered from the plane wreckage this morning."

Needle Stalk

Alexandra Self

Rachel laid down on the acupuncturist's table. When Rachel met Serene, there came a feeling that this woman was familiar to her. But Rachel had never met anyone with the name Serene before, so maybe this woman had a doppelganger in the city. Rachel had never gone to an acupuncturist nor even heard of acupuncture. Rachel's friend told her how the needles make your body produce adenosine, which acts like a local anesthetic. Rachel figured she might as well give it a shot and looked up the nearest acupuncture businesses. After all, the worst that could happen was too many mini stabbings.

Rachel was strapped down by cloth-covered chains. Serene said this was for protection as some patients have reacted negatively and punched her in the face. Rachel thought this was an extreme measure but went along with it because this was Serene's business, so she made the rules.

"Are you doing anything after this appointment?" Serene asked as she inserted the first needle into Rachel's forehead. As Rachel was thinking that her friend was either a filthy liar or her pain receptors were dull, Rachel answered. "My husband, Don, and I are going to go to the adoption agency. We've have been looking forward to being parents for quite a while."

"Oh, so you can have a child while keeping things nice and tight down there?" Serene forced the second needle into Rachel's elbow.

Rachel gritted her teeth. "No, it's not important to us if the child is biological. There are so many children out in the world that need to be adopted."

"Well, if I had a Don in my life, I wouldn't be selfish by thinking about keeping the fetus structure inside me untouched. No, I believe you're not truly in love with him unless you sacrifice your body and have his seed blossom in you." Serene embedded the third needle into Rachel's hand.

Rachel bit her lip and felt like she'd swallowed jagged diamond studs. "I suppose that's one way of looking at things. I'm sorry but I think you're going way too hard."

"This is all part of the process. You must give it time."

"What about you?" said Rachel. "Do you have any kids?"

"No, I never really had much of a boyfriend before, and I don't want to be a single mother." Serene implanted the fourth needle inside Rachel's chin.

Pain enveloped Rachel as if her very soul was wounded. "I heard the bar two blocks away does trivia night. You could look around for speed dating events. You could do a cooking class. Maybe join some free adult hangout groups. Do whatever makes you happy."

"I can never be happy. Not while you are around." Serene stuck the fifth needle into Rachel's neck.

Rachel felt a burn in her throat like she'd drank a thousand glasses of tequila at once. "I'm sorry?"

"You see, you stole Don away from me." The sixth needle was now injected into Rachel's thigh.

Rachel held back her rage-filled tears caused by the pain. "You must have me confused with someone else. I have never met a Serene in my life."

"Oh no, you have met me. When we were in high school. I went by the name Donna as I figured this would make Don like me more."

Rachel had sudden flashbacks of Don complaining about how Donna would steal his used tissues, had a statue of him made of gum pieces, went to prom with polaroids of him stitched into her dress, burned her skin to give herself scars to match Don's birthmarks, cut off and ran away with his dog's leg when she stalked his house, and had to be escorted out of his workplace when she threw a bear trap towards his foot.

Donna said, "Don told me that he would consider me to be his girlfriend if I could put a stop on my 'craziness' as he called it. For a whole month, I was proper and acted completely normal. Then you moved here, and he fell for you instantly even though I am much prettier than you. After that, he had no interest in me. So, I did whatever I could to get his attention again." Serene filled Rachel's stomach with the seventh needle. "I'm sure once you're out of the way, Don will see that I'm the one he's meant to be with."

Rachel felt her blood vessels snap. She struggled against the holds. "You let me out right now or I will massacre you."

"Don't bother your silly, stupid brain. The effects should be settling in now."

Rachel looked down. Her fingers began melting away like lava. Her knee popped out of its sockets. Her insides burned as if formaldehyde had been shot up into her veins. She caught the whiff of her new body scent: rotting flesh. She tasted like she used arsenic for mouthwash. Her bones made a rattling sound. She felt like worms were coming out of her teeth. Her guts made headway towards the floor. Her eyelids disappeared completely. Her tongue bloated like a corpse's. She grew a rat's tail. Rachel screamed.

"Once my concoction has completed its course, you will look as ugly as you have made me feel."

1521 Magnolia

Gina G

The view was blurry, but he could tell he was in a drab green room that smelled like bleach. A large black TV screen faced him from on top of a dresser, and an olive-green chair stood in the corner with a jacket or robe draped over it. There was a window to his right with a single square of blue from outside, a door to the left of the dresser, and a nightstand next to the bed with a book on it and glasses. Objects were easier to identify. They were things he was used to: floor, ceiling, bed, and chair. He put the glasses on, and the fuzziness cleared away.

This was not home.

The door opened, and a woman wearing a blue outfit entered. Her hair was pulled back. A clipboard was tucked under one arm, and she carried a small tray with a glass of water and a medicine cup filled with pills.

"Good morning, Mr. Halloway." She had a friendly voice.

He now knew it was morning, and his name was Mister Halloway.

She set the tray down and said, "And how are we this morning, Henry?

"Henry." He cocked his head to the side and tasted the word, Henry. Mister Henry Halloway. "My name is Henry … Henry Halloway." His voice was shaky.

"Yes, and I'm your nurse Kasi." She handed him the glass of water and pills. "Let's take these and prepare you for the day." Dutifully, he swallowed. "Hand, please." She took his pulse. His movements were mechanical, as though his body recognized the commands before his mind did.

She guided him to the bathroom and straightened his room while he busied himself with the routine listed on the mirror. "Wash hands, brush teeth, take a shower. Press the button if you need help." He followed the instructions. The routine was a guide to help his mind, a trail he could mentally walk down each day. He completed the list, and Nurse Kasi helped him get dressed.

There was a knock on the door, and Kasi turned. "Come in," she said.

"Am I interrupting?" asked a young man with brown hair.

He looked familiar, and Henry sorted through his mental drawers, searching for an identity. He opened the one labeled family, and a memory sifted through of his son, Tom, holding a crying, red-faced little boy out to him and saying, "Here's your grandson, Dad."

"Calvin?"

"Yes!" A smile illuminated the young man's face. "I am your—"

"My Grandson," Henry said, "You've grown up."

"Yes, I'm twenty-five now." Calvin looked to the Nurse. "How is he today?"

"Good," she replied.

Calvin held a newspaper. "Look at this, Grandpa." He pointed to the front page. "They're going to tear down the building you used to own. 1521 Magnolia, right? You grew up in apartment 3D, right?"

Kasi looked over Calvin's shoulder. "It's about time," she said. "That place has been an eyesore for years. Are they putting in a shopping center?"

"Apartments with shops on the main floor. My dad took it

over when Grandpa couldn't... well, you know. Dad finally sold the place six months ago."

Henry took the newspaper and stared at the picture. It was grainy and pebbled and showed a three-story building with run-down bricks, boarded-up windows, and a sagging entryway. Graffiti was sprayed across in a snarl of words on its walls.

The building was old. It had been old when he lived there with his brother Charlie and their mother, Maureen. They moved in after his father was killed in action during World War II. A snippet of memory sifted through his brain, a thread from the past playing out clearly, and he could see himself standing in the doorway with their belongings packed in boxes. His mother was tired and thin from working long hours at the factory. The rooms were small and dingy, the walls peeled, and the kitchen window was cracked open. It never would seal shut.

"It's just till we get back on our feet," his mother said, ruffling his hair as she put on a brave face.

His brother, Charlie, trying hard to be the man of the house, picked up a box and said, "We'll be all right, mama. Come on, Henry, let's go unpack."

They shared a room just big enough for two thin beds and a rickety dresser, at the end of an unlit hallway. No matter what they did, the room stayed cold.

Another memory stole in, taking over with a swish of a curtain fall. It was the first Christmas since his father's death. Three little newspaper-wrapped presents were on the table under a small branch of a tree decorated with ribbons. His mother set out plates of leftover ham the neighbors had given her. The dinner was scarcely enough for one, let alone three, but they made it work. She read from the Bible and pointed out the window to the stars.

"See how bright the North Star is? Do you know what that

means?"

"No." Henry was a wide-eyed wonder of nine years old.

"It means Santa Claus is on his way, and you need to go to bed."

He ran to the little room, filled with the magical hope of Santa Claus bringing his father home, praying for a miracle that would never come true. He awoke shortly after midnight. Charlie lay fast asleep in his bed. The moon left a sliver of silver on the floor, and Henry crept on quiet feet down the hall to the kitchen. The single bulb over the table was still on. Peering around the corner, Henry saw his mother hunched over, shoulders shaking, silent tears falling, holding a picture of his father in her hands.

And then another thread, this one darker, twisted, of a brutal little man … Roger O'Grady, a bow-legged, whip-thin man with a mean streak that came out when he drank too much. Henry could see him standing under the swinging single bulb, a broken piece of wood in his hand, his mother crying on the floor. And a pan. The pan was in Henry's hand, and it was covered with blood.

He twitched and opened his hands to drop the pan, but nothing was there. Everything was different. He was in a room with a bed and a chair. A woman in a blue uniform was talking to someone who looked like his brother.

"Charlie?" he said. "Why are the police here? Did they find the body?"

"Charlie?" The woman in the uniform asked.

"Body?" The man who looked like Charlie cocked his head to one side, like a dog Henry used to have.

"Who's Charlie?" The woman took out a notepad and started writing.

"His brother," the man explained. "He died in Vietnam." He turned to Henry and said slowly, "Grandpa, it's me, Calvin, your grandson."

"Grandson?" Henry shook his head. He took a step back. Something was wrong. Maybe it was a trap to get him to confess.

"Grandpa?" The person who wasn't his brother reached for him.

Henry swatted his hands away. "Don't touch me."

"Easy, Henry." The woman set the notepad down and picked up a syringe. They were going to drug him.

"What do you think you're doing?" Henry moved for the door. The blue-clad woman grabbed his arm. The strangely familiar man held him as she poked him with the needle. He let out a cry and tried to get away. Everything spun in a circle.

"It's okay, Henry, just calm down," she said.

The man helped him to the bed. Henry lay back. "The ground was soft in the corner… it was easier to dig … I didn't mean .. " his voice trailed off, and he fell asleep.

"What was he talking about?" Calvin asked.

Kasi gently plumped a pillow and eased it under Henry's head. "I have no idea. Burying a body? That's weird."

Calvin chewed the edge of his lip. "Do you think I upset him by showing him the picture?"

Kassi said, "I don't think it was the newspaper."

"But he was so focused on it." Calvin ran a hand through his hair.

"These things happen with the disease. Sometimes, patients confuse movies or things they might have seen on television with something similar to their past. The brain is a magnificent piece of machinery, but when it becomes scrambled, it can create all sorts of images that may or may not have existed."

Calvin patted his grandfather's hand and nodded his head. "Do you think he might have killed someone?" he asked her.

Henry was back in his childhood, sitting in his room reading a book and listening to Mom and Roger argue. It was like a record that repeated over and over.

His mom had started dating Roger after they moved into the dingy apartment at 1521 Magnolia. Roger was nice occasionally but could go either way, depending on the booze. On this night, though, Henry could already tell it would go badly. His mother was doing her best to keep things smooth, but he recognized the edge, the crazy in Roger's voice, and knew it was best to stay out of the way. He shut his door, scrunched close to the far wall, and wished Charlie was home. Charlie would know how to handle things. Picking up a comic book, he tried to lose himself in the story when he heard his mom make a wounded sound like an animal in a trap.

"Ow, stop Roger, please!"

Henry looked up from his book.

"You're hurting me." A sob.

Something broke. He heard it shatter. It was followed by his mother pleading.

"Please, Roger, don't…"

"You back-talking me now?" Roger's words slurred.

"No, Roger."

A slap echoed loudly in the small apartment, and Henry jumped. His mom called out. She was scared. He could hear it in her voice.

Another crash—something heavier, like furniture. His mother screamed. The sound pierced his soul and jarred him off the bed like he'd sat on a knife.

"You're going to do what I say bitch, or I'll really hurt you," Roger hissed, low and mean like a poisonous snake.

The kitchen seemed a mile away. Henry crept into the hallway, hearing his mother crying, broken sobs falling like bits of China to the floor. Drawing a breath, he hoped the air would fill him with courage.

He stepped into the kitchen. Roger's sweat-stained back was to him. His mother was tucked into herself like an animal, trying to find shelter. One of her shoes was off, and he could see it lying under the table. A broken chair rested against the stove. Roger brandished one of the legs like a baseball bat above his mom's figure. Time slowed down. Henry took it all in – the broken chair leg descending on his mom, her cries like a baby bird, Roger snarling. Henry did the only thing he could. He grabbed the pot with the stew on the stove and swung it. Roger was crouched over. The pot was heavy –cast iron –and it hit with a resounding thunder that rippled up Henry's arm. It all happened at once. His mother screamed. The chair leg thwacked. The pot struck home, and Roger let out a grunt before slumping to the floor. Henry hit him once more and stood panting over the body. Stew splattered the walls and floor.

"What the hell?" Charlie said from the door.

And Henry turned to face him when everything switched.

"Grandpa?"

Henry was in a green room that smelled like antiseptic. He didn't recognize it, yet it seemed familiar.

"Charlie?"

"No, it's Calvin, Grandpa, your grandson."

"Calvin." The young man seated next to him looked familiar. For a moment, sharp clarity focused his mind, and Henry leaned over to his nephew, whispering, "I killed him in self-defense. He was hurting my mom."

"Who, Grandpa?"

"Roger." His vision grew cloudy again, like a fog was filtering through the room, and his mind walked down a hallway filled with doors. He didn't know which one to open.

"Grandpa?" Calvin's voice came from the end of the hall.

Henry took a deep breath and closed his eyes. When he opened them, he was looking at his grandson, clutching a newspaper in his hands. He remembered newspapers used to leave ink stains on his fingers. Glancing down, Henry saw the picture of the house he grew up in. The one where Charlie helped him bury the body. The one they lived in until he was twelve. Times were different back then. Henry shook his head, and fog fought with his memories. Who was he? Voices were making noise nearby. He could see shapes, but they were out of focus. The sounds he heard were not a song. He tried to sort things out and could almost understand but it was too thick, gray, and foggy.

"U washna gaw walsh granshaw?"

The shape reached for him, and Henry flung out an arm. "I don't know you. Don't touch me." It was what he wanted to say. He could see the words, but the only sound that came out was, "Ash don wa! Doash to maw."

The shape stepped away and faded before coming into focus. It was his older brother. "Charlie." Henry smiled, and the words were clear. He remembered his brother. "Can we get an ice cream? I saved some change."

"Sure, Grand-- Henry. Just give me a moment."

"Okay." Henry leaned back on the bed and watched the black screen play back the nothing in his mind.

Calvin watched his Grandpa stare at the empty screen. What did he see on there? Where was his mind? Calvin glanced at Kassi as she checked his Grandpa's pulse and got him comfortable.

"He's getting worse," he said.

"We feel he is moving into stage six." The nurse kept her gaze at the ground, clutching her clipboard close. "All signs point to that."

"What do we do?"

"There's nothing we can do. It's like they regress and become children again. We can only care for them and keep them comfortable."

"Do you think there was anything to that story he said? About the body?"

She shrugged, "Who knows?"

Calvin nodded like he could understand, but truthfully, the disease scared the shit out of him. It terrified him. Cancer was one thing, Parkinson's another, but to have your mind stolen from you, all your memories, your ability to function, to speak, to lose all of it and be able to do absolutely nothing about it was horrifying.

He forced a smile. "So, is it okay to bring him a milkshake tomorrow?"

Kasi's face brightened, "I think he would like that."

"Strawberry," Calvin said, "that's what I will get him. Would you like one?"

"Oh no, no, no, I'm okay."

He chose not to press the conversation. Instead, he shook her hand and returned to his car, puzzling over his grandfather's words. Outside, it was a perfect postcard day, with light clouds floating like fluffy ships across the horizon and a breeze smelling of spring, soft and dewy with aliveness. Calvin unlocked the door to his Civic, sat down, and rubbed his temples; the Alzheimer's gene ran in his family. He'd been tested and didn't have it. But what if his future children did? It was why he'd chosen to go into the medical field. He wanted to find a cure. Pulling out of the parking lot, his mind mulled over the conversation with his Grandpa, sifting through the story. On a whim, he drove out to the old building on Magnolia Street.

Construction signs kept traffic on one side while workers milled around like orange-vested ants in hard hats. The building seemed to sag in on itself, like it had given up and knew its demise was inevitable. Its windows were broken or boarded up with plywood, eyes closed and empty of life. The doorway lurched to one side, hanging on a single hinge, a gap-toothed opening to a narrow hallway littered with yesterday's trash. Graffiti scarred its façade – angry, stupid words made the building seem bullied and picked on. There was a weight to it, a sorrow, and if it could have talked, he imagined it would have cried tears. Had it ever been a happy place? In all the time he'd known it, the neighborhood had been crime-ridden. Clearly, the mayor was trying to clean it up.

Calvin parked his car and walked over to the building. A couple of the hard hats glanced up at him before continuing their work. He stepped past one of the barriers, nudged a small pile of debris out of the way, and put his hands on the wall. The brick crumbled like heartache at his touch. What secrets did the structure hold? What stories could it tell? Was there a body buried in its roots?

"Hey buddy, you okay?" One of the workers approached him, pants dusted with pulverized bricks and his eyes hidden behind protective glasses.

"Yeah," Calvin brushed his hand on his pant leg. "My Grandpa grew up in this building."

"Oh yeah?" The man replied.

Calvin could tell he didn't really care and was just being polite. He was probably wondering who the crazy guy was who would approach a demolition site.

"When is it coming down?"

"Tomorrow or the next day."

Calvin nodded, letting the thought sink in. "You search the buildings first, right? Before you tear them down? In case something was missed or left? Like a treasure? Old notebooks?" A body hidden in the cellar.

"You thinking we missed something?"

Calvin shook his head. "I'm just asking." He could only reveal so much. "How many buildings are coming down?"

"Two others, the one across the street and next door. Going to make some condo units with shops on the ground floor."

"Should be good for the neighborhood."

"Better than what's been here." The contractor scratched his belly and glanced at his watch.

"Out of curiosity, did you check the cellar for anything?" Calvin did his best to keep his voice neutral.

"I don't handle that part. You'd have to check with the foreman."

"Do you have his number?" The worker rattled off a cell number, and Calvin saved it on his phone, thanking him for his time. He took one last look at the decrepit, dying building and walked back to his car. Once seated, he let the A/C cool him before driving to the police station. It was the only way he could calm his concern. If there were a body, they would take it from there. If there wasn't... well, he'd done his part.

Two weeks later, Calvin was seated in his home office reviewing his bills when Detective Jaylene Rice called him back. They'd found a body.

"Did your grandfather happen to mention any names other than Rogers?" Rice asked.

"No, just the one," Calvin replied. "Why?"

"Well, we found three bodies in the cellar."

"Three?"

111

"Yes," she said, "We would like to talk to your grandfather."

"He has Alzheimer's," Calvin explained, "Stage five right now, moving into six."

"It's a long shot, Mr. Halloway," Rice said. "We're simply hoping to clarify some information."

Legally, Calvin could not prevent them from talking to his grandfather. He didn't think anything would come of it, but what could hurt to ask? His grandfather had gotten steadily worse each time Calvin went to see him. Some days, he could function, and his eyes would announce he was there; other days, he was gone, the light inside him vacant, turned off. Calvin hated those days.

He called the hospital and arranged a time for the detectives to come by.

Henry was in a world of billowing clouds —he floated among them, feeling the faint touch like the lightest stroke of a feather. He had no sense of time, no sense of where he was or even who he was. He heard voices and saw objects, but they drifted in and out of a fog. Words were balloon-like fragments attached to strings he wanted to reach for but couldn't understand. Sometimes, the confusion made him mad, but mostly, he didn't care; he simply floated. Every once in a while, he would come back, and objects would make sense, people would stand out, and he would swim in a pool of memories, but those moments were happening less and less.

"Grandpa?"

The word was familiar, and the sound was something he remembered. The speaking face smiled at him, and he smiled back. A moment of clarity broke through the gray. "Calvin." He remembered his grandson and clapped his hands.

Two other figures stood next to his grandson. They were

dressed in blue suits and held police badges. One had a female build, and the other was stocky and broader in the shoulders. They'd come for him.

"Grandpa, this is Detective Rice and Detective Banks. They have some questions for you."

The female sat down next to him. "Mr. Halloway, we found Roger's body."

Roger. The first body. A memory drifted from the wisps of his mind of Roger beating his mom. Henry hit him with a frying pan. Its swing replayed in slow motion, arching out, coming down, connecting, and the sound was like a cantaloupe being dropped on the floor. When he looked down, Roger lay at his feet, blood seeping from the back of his head. He deserved it.

"Blood," Henry said in the present, but he was seeing the little boy he once was standing, staring at the prone, crumpled body. He dropped the pan, and it fell, clattering to the floor, dancing back and forth before it settled. And then Charlie walked in, took in the scene, and checked the body.

"He's dead," Charlie said. "We have to bury him."

The memory winked out like a camera flash, and Henry looked at his grandson and the detectives. They were detectives. His mind juddered like a stuck engine, and he fought to bring it back. He needed to be sharp and guarded. How much did they know? Had they found the other bodies? He leaned close and whispered, "Charlie said if we told anyone, I could be sent to jail, so we dragged the body to the cellar. We dug a hole in the corner and agreed to tell anyone who asked about Roger that he left town. He was a drifter, no family, and no one cared if he was gone."

"Did you kill Roger O'Grady?" the woman asked.

"It was self-defense," Henry replied.

"There were two other bodies. Do you know anything about

those?" The larger shape stood over him. "Mr. Halloway?"

"Bodies?" Henry wrinkled his brow. "How many?"

"Two," the man repeated. "Should there be more?"

Henry swallowed. Tread carefully, he told himself. He remembered the bully from school, the one who picked on him. He lured the kid into the cellar… And the riots. There were riots when the union went on strike. Everyone was marching down the streets when the police came. He argued with a man. They hid in the alley. The man… got in his face. He hit the bully with a bat he'd hidden by the stairs. There was blood … dirt under his fingernails from digging.

Henry shook his head. The space swam in shades of green. Where was he?

"Grandpa?"

Henry glanced around the green room. Was his grandfather here? Who was talking to him? There was a young man who looked like his brother. There were two people dressed in blue. He couldn't make out their faces. They didn't appear to be smiling. Blue was the color of the ocean. The sky. And fog rolling in. No, fog wasn't blue. Fog was …and inside his mind, the lights went out.

"Grandpa? Do you remember?"

Henry leaned back. Figures were in the fog. The blue ones watched him. They had sharp teeth. They wanted to lock him away in a box.

"Grandpa, do you remember the apartment at 1521 Magnolia?"

It was a rundown building, tired and old. The apartment was small, and the cellar had a dirt floor. He buried three bodies in that cellar – bodies he needed to keep secret. Why were they buried? Wrinkling his brows, Henry tried to remember, and everything was muddy, frayed, and foggy. He tried to cast a line into the lake of his mind and bring it back, but it drifted away.

He was in a room. It had green walls and smelled like bleach. A green blob was next to the bed, and two blue shapes were standing in front of him. They were smiling. Henry liked smiles. They reminded him of balloons.

$\mathcal{H}$eaven-born $\mathcal{W}$ind

Eric John Anderson

Remember the wedding, Mom? You spent all night working on Gretel's little pink dress. She looked like an angel, ruffling the pleats and playing with the taffeta. Hansel too was adorable in that little gray suit with the little pink tie. It stayed clean for most of the ceremony, at least. After John and I said our vows and after the cake and dancing, Hansel looked up in my eyes and you know it only took three years of dating their father, he finally called me "momma" for the first time!

God, it feels like an oven in here. Can I open a window?

There, that feels better.

I'm trying to remember if you offered to take the kids before or after John got sick. It was definitely after the news started spouting off about virus-this and second-COVID that. I remember calling you and panicking. You said, "Don't worry about the things you can't control."

You told me the first day was rough. I texted you and asked how it was going. You sent back something like, "Gretel is learning to cross-stitch, but Hansel is angry he can't go home and watch YouTube." Boy, was that an understatement.

He stole your phone and snuck out with Gretel, using the map to find his way home. I was furious when they showed up at the door. John didn't understand why. Of course, I was relieved that both of them were okay, but they really shouldn't have been around John with his fever. I get that they're his kids, but they really put themselves—and you—in danger. Just like when...

You welcomed them back with open arms. No harm done. Your ever-present forgiving nature shined through as you said, "Who has brought you here, my darlings!" You always have a funny way with words.

Are you feeling comfortable enough? I know it's hard to breathe. And dammit, why is this room so hot? It's the only room we could fit the medical bed into, but I wish we could get you back in your own bed. Hansel hated sleeping in here. He said he felt like he was locked in a stable. I don't know where he gets that from, probably all that YouTube he watches. That first night, he lasted maybe an hour before crawling into bed with you. Every night was a cuddle session with grandma after that. Did you say that Gretel started crawling into bed with you as well? They really do love you, Mom.

I think once you're feeling better, John should bring some of his carpenter buddies and work on your house. The roof and siding could use some updating, they look like a seventies gingerbread fever dream. I'm surprised the kids didn't nibble on the windowsills.

Of course, you know we wouldn't do anything unless you wanted us to. I know how much it means to you that Dad designed the house. We don't want you to think we are trying to spend your money.

Actually, Mom, can we talk about that? Well, it's hard for you to talk, I know. I'll just keep rambling. I don't even know if you can hear me. I know Dad left you with enough money, but I'm really concerned about your jewelry and pearls. The antique ones like Grandma's pendant and brooch. I don't want to think what Becky would do... You know, I've always felt she had some strange sibling rivalry going on with me in her head. She would probably sell everything off the minute your will is read just to spite me. I want it to stay in the family. Maybe you could bequeath it to Gretel once the adoption papers are filed. It'd be nice to pass something on to my kids that means so much to me. Us. Well, step-kids, but you know what I mean.

It was so hard trying to get pregnant with "he-who-must-not-be-named." Total f-ing nightmare. Sorry, didn't mean to use impolite language with you, Mom, but I seriously had given up on the thought of ever being a mother. And you never thought you would ever be a grandma, but look at you now!

We don't have to talk about money right now, I know you're in pain. I just want you to think it over. Your lips are dry, let me grab some ice.

The second time Hansel and Gretel snuck out, they couldn't find your phone. I just found it in your pantry, you must have hidden it high up on the shelf where they couldn't reach it. I don't know what they were thinking that night. Maybe Hansel thought he could figure out the way back to our place. Who knows, maybe he left breadcrumbs along the way. Ha!

They gave me quite a fright, getting lost in the woods. I'm sure they were also pretty scared.

Gretel eventually told me what happened out there that night. They walked deeper and deeper into the woods, further than they'd ever been. They didn't recognize anything. Gretel wanted to return to your house, but Hansel got distracted by a large snow-white bird sitting high on a branch. They followed it from tree branch to tree branch until it started getting dark. Once they realized they were lost, they gathered up a bunch of brush-wood—like John taught them to do on our many campouts. Lord knows where Hansel got the matches, but I tell you what, he's grounded until college. I promise you that.

This is the part that really shook me. Gretel said they were sitting on the ground, watching the fire grow higher and higher into the canopy of trees. Sparks of embers flying up and dying

like fireflies into the night sky. They were huddled together, trying to stay warm. In the darkness of the thicket, a pair of shimmering eyes appeared and came near.

She talked about how the eyes belonged to a dark figure of
a man who approached their fire cautiously. His features were
sallow and shriveled. They were both frightened of him until he
spoke. His voice was slow and smooth. They felt like they weren't
in any danger. He came near and sat beside the fire and asked
them if they had any food.

Gretel had the foresight of bringing some bread along; she
had stolen some of your famous sourdough. She dug it out of
her little plastic purse and offered it to the man. She actually
didn't call him a man when she was trying to describe him, it
seemed like he was something otherworldly. She had a hard time
trying to decide if he was a ghost or just some homeless guy who
saw the light of the fire.

He took a few bites of bread but then scowled as if it was
rotten and gave it back. After staring into the fire for a few more
minutes, he got up and without a word, left them. If we ever find
out who it was, he is going to get an earful from me. Who would
just leave a pair of lost children out in the woods by themselves?
The nerve of some people.

Anyway, Mom, this is what I need to tell you. I think Gretel
may have given Hansel some of the bread the stranger had taken
a bite out of. I think the man was sick, and, I'm so sorry, Mom,
but I think Hansel may have brought this virus home to you. I
know you don't like us making a fuss about you, but here you
are, struggling to breathe. Machines hooked up all around you. I
want to pull you out of here, rip out all these damn wires out. It's
killing me to watch you go through this. Every rasping breath is
cutting through me with steel blades.

Of course I would never let him know what happened, but I

think he may have an inkling that he infected you. If it takes my whole life, I will never let him believe that of himself.

Geez, why is this room so hot?

Are you still with me, Mom?

Mom?

> *'Nibble, nibble, gnaw,*
> *Who is nibbling at my little house?'*
> *The children answered:*
> *'The wind, the wind, The heaven-born wind,'*
> *- The Brothers Grimm*

The Groom

Pat Partridge

Peter, at thirty-four, was on his third job since graduation, owned a decent condo, and liked Marvel movies. He was also engaged again. In two weeks, he would marry Jocelyn, a woman whose looks and brains far surpassed any expectations he'd had for a life partner, so much so that even his father believed he was "marrying up." Peter hated the expression, but he couldn't disagree. It should have made him happy. Or at least happier. Not so much. Happiness stayed remarkably elusive.

Ordinary had ordinarily been good enough for Peter. For years he drove a Ford pickup and changed the oil himself. He liked to fish and owned a shotgun. He drank beer that came in cans. He'd kissed a girl when he was eleven, felt one up when he was fifteen, got laid at eighteen. He'd mowed lawns when he was fourteen and later spent three summers working shitty construction jobs. He had a favorite football team—the Saints—and on his bookshelf, he displayed a plastic-encased baseball signed by Hall of Famer Jim Palmer that his dad gave him as a high school graduation present. It was worth over a hundred bucks now, but he couldn't bring himself to Ebay it.

He'd gone to college, but nothing about it inspired him. He majored in computer science because his dad insisted he study something practical, which turned out to be okay. But that was all it was. Practical. Like brushing one's teeth twice a day. He rooted for his school's football and basketball teams, played intramural soccer, and wore a cap with the school insignia on it. He couldn't bring himself to join an expensive fraternity—not practical, his dad said—but he was good looking and sociable and was often invited to frat parties where he was regularly called upon to be a designated driver. Which was fine with Peter; he liked being asked to help others.

He met his first fiancé, Roberta, at a Deke frat party his senior year, and they hit it off right away. Sitting on one of the beer-stained sofas, the music blaring, they somehow managed to make each other laugh. When they got onto the dance floor, she smiled as he attempted to move his body to the beat.

He got up close and said, "You're a good dancer."

"You too," she said.

That was all it took to fall in love. A little later, during a slow dance, his body tight against hers, his pal-in-his-pants showed an interest, and Roberta's eyebrows went up in response. She grinned and winked.

They were engaged in April of their senior year and planned to marry in August at the chapel on the campus. It was all so sensible. Reasonable. Positive. A tech company had offered him a job—his dad's advice having paid off—and he was ready to get on with his future. He started to imagine a path forward for his life, one with bright, if poorly defined, prospects.

But the path diverged quickly. The day he and Roberta graduated, they spent the afternoon together with their families. His dad said Roberta seemed "practical, grounded," said she would "make a great wife and mother." Peter agreed. His dad was usually right about things like that, and it made him happy to have his dad's blessing. Two days later, Roberta called off the wedding.

"What happened?" Peter asked. He was baffled, not angry.

"You don't love me enough." She avoided looking into his eyes, preferring to focus on the prized baseball on his bookshelf.

"Enough for what?"

"Enough to make it work."

"What's it?"

"Us."

Later, Peter ran into Julie, Roberta's intended maid-of-honor, at the Safeway. He'd heard she had a falling out with Roberta, which must have been true because Julie immediately commiserated with him. She said the engagement failing wasn't his fault, it was Roberta's. And Roberta's dad. Her father had questioned her choice of husband, had told her, "You can do better."

Two years later, Roberta sent Peter an invitation to her upcoming wedding. Why? Out of pity? Or spite? He didn't attend, preferring not to know if she'd done "better."

By thirty-four, Peter had casually abandoned any pretense of grandiose plans. That surprised no one, least of all himself. But he didn't complain. Two years earlier, he'd landed a great job, had done well, and had been promoted twice. His take-home was fifty percent higher than the day he started. That was nothing to sneeze at, his dad said. Peter's natural instinct to help others was the proverbial feather in his cap at a company that attracted its share of aspiring assholes. His boss, a woman named Marie, called him her "wing man," which made the other guys chuckle. They considered Peter a suck-up, but he thought that was unfair.

He worked out at the gym three days a week, grew a beard but soon abandoned it. He bought a car—a "gently used" BMW—that, much to his surprise, improved his online dating prospects. Who knew?

He met Jocelyn Orville on Match.com. She was single, again. Two years earlier, she'd ended a four-year marriage to a guy who was, she said, "a complete jerk." Peter didn't doubt it, but he didn't ask many questions, preferring not to compare himself to the jerk.

Jocelyn, thirty-one and still a head-turner, came from a prosperous background, had a master's degree in business management, and worked for a company that planned to go public. That, she said, would put "real money" in her bank account. She drove a BMW too. Her dad gave it to her when she finished graduate school.

"I like your style," she told him on their second date.

It pleased him to know he had a style.

On the third date, they went to bed and the sex was wonderful. She said she liked his style there too. It was a nice compliment, but he didn't care for the added pressure.

Jocelyn was smart in ways Peter appreciated. She was educated, cultured. One night when they were in bed together after making love, she asked him a question about literature. He had not expected that line of inquiry. He'd been looking at her muscled legs, impressed at how little cellulite they showed.

"Have you read Hemingway's story, The Short Happy Life of Francis Macomber?" she asked.

"What's it about?"

"About a man and his wife on safari in Africa. He finally comes alive while hunting a rhino."

"How does it end?"

"You'll have to read it. It's a masterpiece."

"Hemingway wrote To Have and Have Not, right?"

Her eyes lit up. "Yes. But I've never read it."

Peter enjoyed the moment. "It's about a man who reluctantly gets involved with the French Resistance." He hadn't read the book, only seen the movie version on Turner Classics late one night, but he skipped over mentioning that. It starred Humphrey Bogart as the reluctant hero, and, if Peter remembered right, it didn't end well for the "have nots."

The more Jocelyn introduced Peter to new things—books,

plays, whatever—the more Peter felt like his life was opening up. Like his horizon was getting wider, the sky bluer. Even his dreams changed. He stopped having the recurring dream about walking down a desolate trail in a forest. His life became exciting, uncomfortable.

This time, when Peter met Jocelyn's parents, things went better than they had with Roberta's family. Jocelyn's dad fished, and he and Peter spent a day on Lake Jackson, drank Heinekens, and caught the limit. Peter landed two lunkers.

"You're a damn good fisherman," her dad said.

"No, just lucky today, Mr. Orville."

"Don't undersell yourself, Peter." He put a hand on Peter's shoulder. "Call me Phil."

Jocelyn introduced Peter to her friends, both male and female. A few of the men sported Rolexes, but they treated him as an equal, or something close enough. The women had perfectly coiffed hair with blonde highlights. Jocelyn said they were jealous because she dated the best-looking guy. Peter didn't fit in with her friends like a gentleman's hands in fine leather gloves— he didn't own fine leather gloves anyway—but the two of them were invited to parties and weekend outings. He made sure they arrived in his BMW freshly washed. He mostly had a good time; certainly nothing to complain about. His dad expressed immense satisfaction in his new girlfriend. "Just don't blow it," he advised.

They dated for six months. On a walk through the botanic gardens in June, the lilies in bloom, he suggested they stop at a wooden bench under a lovely flowering apple tree. Jocelyn breathed deeply, said the scents were "intoxicating."

"The earth laughs in flowers." She picked up a fallen bloom. "It's from a poem by Emerson."

Peter barely heard her, his nerves on edge. He held her hard and said, "I love you deeply." He said a few other things he'd rehearsed and finally asked, "Will you marry me?" He held out a box with a two-carat, princess-cut, all-natural diamond the saleslady at Jared Jewelers said was a "sure winner."

The saleslady was right. Jocelyn said yes. That night, the sex was especially wonderful.

They scheduled the wedding for September, barely enough time for Jocelyn to prepare a perfect second wedding which, apparently, has different rules than for a perfect first wedding. Peter had never experienced a bride-to-be in the flush of matrimonial preparations and quickly concluded to stay out of the way. When asked his opinion about wedding flowers, he'd said he liked pink roses.

"You're kidding, right?" Jocelyn said. "Pink roses are something you'd give your mother."

Peter had never given his mom pink roses. "Okay, how about white?" He knew white was at least appropriate for weddings.

"Boring."

"What do you want?"

"Pale blue."

From then on, when Peter was asked about wedding options—music, food, favors—he smiled and asked, "Which do you like best?" Jocelyn always had an answer.

As the wedding approached, Peter vacillated between elation and terror. He couldn't tell if he was launching a magnificent life he'd assumed was on the far side of impossible or inching toward an unforgiving cliff. It didn't help when his future father-in-law, Mr. Orville—he still had trouble calling him Phil—surprised him with some advice about Jocelyn.

"You know, Peter," he said. He was nursing his second beer while barbecuing on the deck of his large home. "Jocelyn isn't an easy girl to manage."

The word "girl" struck Peter as odd, but even more so, he'd never planned to "manage" Jocelyn.

Mr. Orville continued. "You'll have to be strong, because when she gets up a head of steam, she can steamroll just about anyone. Jocelyn's first husband, Louis, didn't have a chance. Pretty quickly, he quit trying." He tossed his beer bottle into the nearby trashcan. "Jocelyn calls him 'the jerk,' but Louis wasn't such a bad guy, really. He was military, expected something different. Things went downhill fast. Before it was over, they'd learned to hate each other. I know his dad. We go to the same club. He says Louis is still fuming about it."

"Thanks for the advice...Phil. I'm sure we'll be fine. I really love your daughter."

Mr. Orville snickered. "Those were the exact words Louis said when I gave him the same advice." He put a hand on Peter's shoulder and looked him in the eye. "It's gonna take more than love, son. It's gonna take courage."

That night in August, the wedding a month away, Peter wracked his memory for times in his life when he'd been courageous. Not much—actually, nothing—came to mind. Recently, he'd picked up a snake near the swing set in the playground that was scaring the kids, but he already knew it was a harmless garter snake. So that didn't count. He once dodged a car at the last second that drifted across the road into his lane, but that merely took quick reflexes. So that didn't count. His job required attention to detail and persistence and cooperation, not courage. So nothing there. Growing up, he'd never needed to stand up to a bully because he was too big and strong for anyone to bully him. He'd never saved anyone from a burning building or wrestled a knife or gun from someone threatening a loved one.

Courage simply wasn't something Peter could list on his internal resume. It troubled him.

In the final days leading up to the wedding, Peter felt better if not exactly calm. He happily followed directions from Jocelyn, helped when asked, and stayed out of the way at other times. She was a whirling dervish of energy getting things done but pooped out by the end of the day. She showed no interest in sex, and Peter didn't pressure her. Soon, she would be in his bed every night. He could wait.

"You've been a wonderful help," Jocelyn told him the day before the wedding.

"Thank you. I'm glad you let me help." He kissed her cheek. "But you made all the arrangements and made it seem effortless." She liked compliments, especially ones about her competence.

Jocelyn beamed. "Tomorrow, I don't want you to see me until I walk down the aisle. Got it?"

"Sure," he said, grinning. "I'll be stashed away in the groom's room until the last minute." He reached out for her. "But how about right now I get a good look at all of you?"

"Oh, Peter," she said. But she didn't stop him when he started to unbutton her blouse.

Some of the one hundred-and-six guests invited to the wedding, if you included the plus-ones, started arriving before nine-thirty for the ten o'clock event to get preferred seats. Jocelyn had reserved a modest 1920s chapel with Gothic-inspired stained-glass windows and had beautifully decked it out with pale blue chiffon draped from column to column and white candles in tall brass candle sticks along the aisles. Peter hadn't seen the dress, but he knew the church decorations coordinated with her dress, a sleeveless cream silk affair draped with pale blue metallic organza.

A string quartet played songs as guests arrived while Peter hunkered down in the sacristy behind the apse with the minister and best man, Jocelyn's brother Rod.

Peter didn't talk. He was nervous. He wanted everything to go off as planned. He stared at his cell phone. His hands shook. He took a deep breath and typed out a short note, then put it away.

"You aren't the first young man to be nervous on his wedding day," the minister said. "And you won't be the last."

Peter tried to smile. "I know. It's just that I want this day to be perfect for Jocelyn."

"And you too, right?"

"Yes. Me too."

"I'm sure it will be." The minister wasn't much older than Peter, but he clearly saw himself as sensitive and wise. "Just practice your vows."

"Good idea," Peter said. "They're on my cell phone."

The minister laughed. "Better than paper. Phones don't rattle in your hands when you're nervous."

Jodie, the maid of honor, burst into the room through the back door.

"Peter! Come quick! Jocelyn needs you."

"What's wrong?" Peter stood up.

She looked at the other two men. "I think it's better if Jocelyn tells you."

"But what about me seeing the dress?"

"Just come!"

Jodie led the way out of the church, around to the front entrance to the small room where Jocelyn and her three bridesmaids waited.

"Oh, Peter!" Jocelyn practically screamed when she saw him. She thrust herself into his arms for a second but quickly withdrew. "Look!" Her hands trembled as she held out her cell phone.

He looked at the small screen and his eyes grew huge.

"Who sent this?"

"I don't know! It's just a phone number. I don't know it."

"It's got to be a prank," Peter said, but he didn't sound convinced.

"Peter, it's a bomb threat. A bomb threat on my wedding day! Who would do something like that?"

Peter shook his head. "Only a crazy person." He paused. "Maybe it was your ex, Louis?"

"Louis?" Her voice rose, considering the thought.

Peter took her hands in his. "No," he said. "I'm sure he wouldn't do anything that stupid."

Jocelyn's eyes swirled, unable to focus. "What are we going to do?"

He took a breath. "First, we're going to clear the church. But we need to hurry. The note says the bomb will go off sometime around 10:15." He scowled. "Whoever wrote it made it vague to terrify us even more. The asshole!"

"It's almost ten now."

"I know. You and the bridesmaids go outside and stop others from coming in. I will tell the congregation."

Peter gathered his thoughts as he raced to inform the minister and his future brother-in-law, who both immediately headed out the back door. He stepped to the front of the altar. He would have to avoid a stampede, but how?

"Friends and family," he began. "We have a small emergency and need to evacuate the church immediately. Please head to the nearest exit now."

"What's the matter?" It was Jocelyn's dad. He wasn't one to take orders easily.

"Just trust me, Phil," he said. "Jocelyn is waiting for you outside. She can explain when everyone is out." He deepened his voice. "Those of you in the front, please start exiting through the side doors." He pointed toward the doors emphatically.

The crowd grumbled and mumbled but started heading out. No one ran, which was good, but some of the older guests moved dangerously slow.

"Those of you who are young and strong, please help expedite anyone who needs help." He considered his next words. "Even if you have to carry them."

Phil Orville turned back to look at Peter. He saw the seriousness on Peter's face. "Yes, folks. Do as Peter says. Let's hurry."

The last few left the church. It was eerily quiet. Peter looked at his watch. 10:07. The bomber, if there was one, said the bomb would explode "around 10:15." He might have enough time to locate it and save damage to the building.

Where would a clever bomber place it? Not under a pew. Too easy to spot. Somewhere it would hurt Jocelyn. Or him. It had to be on the altar. He glanced around, but he already knew there were few unexposed places. The lectern. The lectern, he knew, had a small cabinet underneath that housed the electronics for the microphone. He looked at his watch. 10:08. He raced over to the lectern and yanked open the door.

There it was. Two sticks of dynamite bound together. Wires extended from them to a small box, an igniter of some kind. He took a deep breath. The digital readout on the box clicked over to 10:09. No time to defuse it, even if Peter knew how.

He carefully picked up the bomb, making sure not to bump the edges of the lectern. He glanced to see if anyone was still in the church. No one. Good. He raced as safely as he could toward the west entrance. Outside was a large dumpster. When he exited, some of the congregants were lingering there, partially blocking his path. A woman screamed when she saw the bomb.

"Hurry to the front of the church!" Peter yelled to the crowd.

"I'm going to the dumpster." He almost tripped as he stepped off the curb onto the parking lot. "Shit!"

He reached the dumpster quickly. The heavy lid was already open. Good. He looked inside. Large green trash bags would soften the landing of the bomb. Also good. He tossed the bomb onto one of the bags, turned, and dashed away.

He stopped twenty yards away and looked at his watch. 10:13. No explosion.

Word spread quickly. A crowd gathered near the front of the church by the street within view of the dumpster. Peter started backing up toward them, his eyes on the dumpster. 10:14. Nothing.

Jocelyn raced up to him. "Oh my god, Peter! You could've been killed!"

She hugged him, but he gently pushed her away. "Not now." It was 10:15. Still nothing. He kept eyeing the dumpster. Off in the distance, sirens, lots of sirens, could be heard approaching. Peter suspected they would not arrive in time to help.

A huge explosion erupted inside the dumpster, flames shooting fifteen feet into the air like the fire breath of a dozen dragons. A moment passed, and trash rained down as far away as the gathered crowd—paper cups, church newsletters, old hymnals, some of them on fire.

It was 10:17. Like the bomber promised, around 10:15.

The dumpster still burned as Phil Orville approached Peter shaking his head. "Son, that was mighty brave." He reached out and put his hand on Peter's shoulder. "But I hope that's the craziest thing you ever do in your life."

"Me too."

His father approached, shaking his head, speechless. He hugged Peter. All he said was, "Wow."

The wedding went on eventually. The bomb squad wouldn't let anyone back inside the church, and the police took a half hour to interview Jocelyn and Peter about what happened. But when the couple, holding hands, said they wanted to go ahead with the wedding, Mr. Orville—Phil—called his country club, who agreed to host an impromptu wedding. Only a handful of guests indicated they wanted to attend. Most wanted to go home and wait to see themselves on the six-o'clock news.

Jocelyn, still in her gorgeous pale blue silk-and-organza wedding dress, rode to the club with her maid of honor in the limo that had been waiting outside the church. Peter took his own car.

He drove slower than normal. Thinking. Soon, he would be married to a beautiful, amazing woman. For life, if all went well. She would probably make more money than him, and she may never want children. They would figure it out. He firmly believed he was finally ready. Nothing would stop him.

He parked his car toward the back of the country club, back behind the kitchen. He took a short walk to the large trash can. He glanced around. No one was watching. He lifted the lid, took a small object out of his pocket, and tossed it in the bin.

He wouldn't need it anymore. He had another cell phone.

Road Trip

Rashelle Yeates

All four of them were feeling wild and free on the third day into their two-week-long road trip. They were excited to find out what life was like outside of the midsized city they called home.

"Aren't you going a little fast?" Lacy leaned forward, looking at Joansie in the rearview mirror.

Joansie grinned back at her, taking her eyes off the dark road in front of them. "Not at all." She pressed down on the pedal, proving she could go faster if she wanted.

Lacy leaned back in the seat, not sure why they allowed Joansie to drive at night. Joansie was crazy, driving like a maniac no matter the time of day. It just seemed worse at night, especially on roads that had no lights.

They were surrounded by blackness, only broken by the occasional passing car. The way Joansie drove never failed to get on Lacy's nerves. She swore she did it on purpose.

Lacy usually enjoyed riding in a car but not when the driver was crazy. Sighing, she stared out into the dark that covered the land.

Evelyn leaned into her shoulder, drawing her attention away from the dark view.

"Don't let her get to you." She spoke low enough so her voice wouldn't carry to the front seat.

Lacy smiled at Evelyn, thankful she had been able to get the time off work to join them on the trip. "I'll try," she said, keeping her voice low.

"Ah, ha." Harley pointed out the front window. "I knew there was a town here."

The two girls leaned forward peering out the front window. They had passed the last town, with a motel, because it had been too early to stop. Lacy's arguments that they could find something interesting to do had fallen on deaf ears. The others didn't want to stop that early.

This part of the country had a whole lot of nothing between small towns that usually only boasted a small motel and a local bar. Why had they decided to come this way? Since Harley put this trip together, she must have a destination in mind. And that was why Joansie was with them as well.

They all stared at the glowing lights in the distance. Most of the small towns had a couple of streetlights in the center of town that the girls couldn't see until they were right on top of it.

"How big is this town supposed to be?" Lacy couldn't believe there was a city in the middle of nowhere big enough to have as many lights on as this one did.

Harley looked down at the map in her lap. Lacy couldn't tell if she was confused or verifying this was the place she thought it was. "Not big enough for so many lights." She chewed on her lower lip. "We didn't take any turns I'm not aware of, did we?"

Evelyn poked her shoulder. "Of course not, you've been awake the whole time."

"Then this is the correct town."

Now Lacy could see the uncertainty beneath the bravado. Harley had always been one to rush into things without thinking. That's what Lacy liked about her. Harley drew her out of her comfortable shell, and Lacy balanced Harley by thinking of the things she didn't. Which she hadn't been able to do for this trip.

"Are you sure?" Joansie squinted at the approaching lights.

Lacy didn't know what she was trying to see, the view was the same.

"Yes." Harley's voice firmed, her stubbornness coming out. Even if the town turned out to be a different one, she would never admit it.

Shaking her head, Lacy looked at Evelyn, who was staring worriedly out the windshield. Laying her hand on Evelyn's arm, she asked, "What's wrong?"

Evelyn looked at Lacy. "This doesn't feel right."

Lacy had never seen Evelyn look so shaken."What feels wrong?"

"I don't know." Evelyn glanced out the window again. "I don't want to stop here. Let's find somewhere else?"

Joansie snapped without looking back, "Absolutely not. It's late, and I'm tired of driving."

"I can drive." Evelyn returned in a small voice.

"This is the town I had planned for us to stop at." Harley's tone was softer, but just as firm as Joansie's. "Huntsville." She pointed to the sign as they passed it.

"What's in Huntsville?" Lacy wasn't sure there was anything of interest there.

"You'll find out in the morning." Harley waved her hand, being vague.

"Why won't you just tell us?"

"Because this must be seen." Harley was stubborn and she wasn't going to change her mind now.

Joansie slowed the car when they got to the edge of town. The lights were everywhere. There weren't many streets, but every road had at least three lights. They lit up the small town like daylight.

Looking around, Lacy tried to figure out what the draw was. She saw the motel, where they were headed, and a few dark-fronted restaurants, but nothing stood out. Harley had some weird ideas when it came to interesting things to see.

The darkness beyond the town was denser and felt more sinister. Like the light was hiding the things waiting in the trees. Lacy shook her head at her runaway imagination. That's what she got from listening to Evelyn.

Checking into the motel went smoothly with the late hour. They settled into their room with sighs of relief. Lacy stretched thankful she wasn't in the car any longer.

Evelyn remained quiet, but Lacy was sure she would be back to normal in the morning. Every situation was worse at night.

Loud banging on the wall above their heads jolted all four girls awake. Lacy sat up and looked over at the others, seeing Joansie also sitting up.

"What was that?" she whispered, feeling like she needed to keep her voice down. The churning in her stomach making her disquiet worse.

"The neighbors are rowdy." Joansie shrugged, laughing, while stretching back out.

Lacy couldn't recall there being a vehicle in the parking space next to theirs. But Joansie must be right. She laid down determined to get more sleep when no more sounds were heard. Lacy wouldn't be able to tolerate Joansie's sass if she were tired, and that wouldn't make for a comfortable trip.

Lacy woke feeling groggy, having slept more deeply than she expected to with the jolt of adrenaline from the middle of the night. Groaning, she pushed up on the bed barely making it to a seated position. Her whole body wanted to flop back down.

"Wh—" Lacy had to swallow a couple of times before her voice would work. "What time is it?"

Nobody answered her.

Looking over her shoulder, she forced her eyes to focus on Harley and Joansie still sleeping in the other bed. She turned to see if Evelyn was awake, but she wasn't in bed.

Lacy listened closely for a few minutes, not realizing she heard nothing from the direction of the bathroom—no water from the shower or sink nor the toilet flushing.

Evelyn wouldn't have left the room by herself, would she? Lacy was sure she would have woken one of them to let them know.

Glancing at the door, she saw the security lock was still engaged. Evelyn couldn't have left with that still locked.

Something was wrong.

Scrambling out of bed, Lacy headed to the bathroom wanting to make sure Evelyn wasn't lying on the floor, hurt and unable to call out for help. Throwing open the door, she found it empty.

Moving to the window, she pushed aside the curtains. The car was still parked where they left it. Nothing was out of place. Nothing but the fact Evelyn wasn't there.

"Harley, wake up." Lacy shook her shoulder knowing how deeply Harley slept.

After ages, Lacy finally got Harley to open her blurry eyes. "What is it, Lacy? I thought we agreed we wouldn't wake the others if they wanted to sleep in."

"Evelyn is gone." Lacy ignored Harley's comment. They had never made that agreement.

"What?" Harley bolted upright. "Did she take the car?"

Of course, Harley was worried about the car. They had borrowed her father's car for the trip. He had threatened mayhem if anything happened to it.

"No, she didn't take the car." Lacy went to where Joansie put the keys last night, holding them up as proof. "And the door is still locked."

"Then she's probably in the bathroom. Jeez, Lacy, stop being so melodramatic." Lacy gripped Harley's arm stopping her from laying back down.

"Melodramatic?" Lacy half screeched. "Don't you think I would have looked in the bathroom before waking you up? It was the first place I looked." Lacy's voice increased in volume with every word until she was yelling.

"Lacy, shut up," Joansie muttered from underneath a pillow on the other side of the bed.

"No," Lacy said as loud as before. "Evelyn's gone, and we need to find her."

Pulling the pillow from her face, Joansie looked at Lacy like she was crazy. "What do you mean 'gone'?"

"Not here, disappeared—what else do you think 'gone' means?" Lacy tossed her hands in frustration. Joansie grunted as she sat up on the side of the bed rubbing her face.

Lacy knew neither one of them were morning people, but they had an emergency on their hands. She thought that would force them into moving at least a little faster.

No such luck.

Lacy got ready for the day knowing that if she was good to go, they wouldn't mess around. She took her time, hoping she wouldn't have long to wait for them. It was hard—in the morning, they were like turtles in the cold. After gathering her things, she carefully collected Evelyn's things also. As soon as they found her, Lacy wanted to leave.

Having packed all their things in the car, Lacy leaned against the front bumper waiting for the other girls to emerge.

"Finally," she muttered, straightening as they came out the door. "I think it'll be best to look around on foot first."

Harley looked at her with worried eyes, but didn't say anything.

"I agree." Joansie stopped next to Lacy, putting one foot up on the bumper.

"Could you please not do that?" Harley stood in front of them.

"Do what?" Lacy asked, confused.

"Lean on the car like that." She pointed to Joansie's foot and Lacy's butt.

"Seriously?" Lacy asked, taking a step away from the car. "That's what you're worried about?"

"Not really," Harley said, stuffing her hands in her pockets. "I focus on the less important things when I'm stressed, okay?"

Joansie straightened away from the car without saying anything. She paced a few steps away, arms folded across her chest. "Where should we begin looking?" she asked without looking at either one of them.

Shaking her head, Lacy looked past the motel parking lot. There were buildings that housed small antique stores, or more likely junk stores, and a few museums depicting what life was like in the area centuries ago.

"Why were you determined to stop here, Harley?" Lacy asked, still searching for any sign of Evelyn.

"I wanted to see the museums," she said in a small voice.

Joansie nodded. All of them were interested in history. That was how they bonded in the beginning. Harley had been the one to draw them together.

It turns out the small town didn't wake up until ten, so they ended up at the only diner. Lacy sat, legs bouncing from impatience to get started on the search for Evelyn. Where had she gone? Why did she leave?

Lacy looked across the table at Joansie and Harley. They sat eating their pancakes. She didn't understand them. Weren't they worried about Evelyn?

What was going on?

It didn't make any sense.

Lacy stared into her coffee, trying to figure this out. This trip had gone to hell so quickly.

"Harley"—she looked up at Lacy expectantly—"what's the draw of these museums in this town?"

Harley shrugged.

"A small town in the middle of nowhere," Joansie grumbled eating the last of her pancakes.

"The middle of nowhere can be fun at times." Harley glared at Joansie. "You didn't want to make the decision of where to go on this trip, so keep your comments to yourself."

Joansie shrugged looking out the window.

"Are you finished with breakfast?"

They nodded, both pushing their plates away. "Then let's pay and find Eve. She's got to be around here somewhere."

They exited the café, blinking in the bright morning light. Where to start? Lacy looked down the block at the different buildings, probably the first museum. Evelyn had always been interested in museums, in the old and in the fantastical.

"Do you think we should split up?" Harley pointed at the three different buildings.

"No." Lacy refused to have anyone go off on their own. "I think we should stick together. Since Evelyn's missing, it would be better to stay together."

"Do you really think that would happen again?" Harley was skeptical.

"It's already happened once, why not again?"

Harley rolled her eyes.

Without commenting on Harley's obvious disdain, Lacy walked to the first museum. It was amazing that such a small town had so many.

Searching all three museums took less than two hours. Standing outside the last one, Lacy fisted her hands to keep them from shaking. "Where do we look now? In the forest?"

"There's still the antique shop." Joansie gestured toward the large building at the end of the street.

"Evelyn doesn't like those kinds of shops."

"It's another place to look." Harley sided with Joansie. "If she's not there, we can look in the forest. Or talk to people. Although everyone we've talked to so far haven't seen her."

"Fine," Lacy stomped off in frustration with the lack of progress.

She could hear the girls muttering behind her but didn't pay attention to what they were saying. She didn't care. All she wanted to do was find Evelyn and get out of there. This trip was over.

Walking into the antique store, she realized it was a lot bigger than it appeared from the outside. There were rows and rows of junk and stuff piled together. She couldn't see very far into the room. In the back corner, she caught a hint of a staircase leading upward. This building was terrible to try to find anything in, let alone Evelyn.

Turning to the other two, Lacy indicated the stairway. "Do we want to start at the top or this floor?"

"Might as well start at the top." Harley moved down the small, twisted path that meandered through the piles of junk to the stairs. "That way we know what we've done and are not passing through more space."

"Ok." Joansie followed Harley stopping here and there to look at items of interest to her. "Can you believe this? Antiques? I don't think so."

Harley led the way up the stairs with Lacy bringing up the rear. By the time she made it to the top, the other two girls were no longer in sight. "Hey! I thought we were staying together."

Silence.

They were playing with her. This was something they would do, even in a situation like this. "Come on Joansie, Harley. This isn't funny."

Still no response.

Sighing with exasperation, Lacy made her way down the left path through the junk. She would start there, and when she ran across the other girls, she would give them a piece of her mind. They were always fooling around, and Lacy could use a laugh, but this wasn't funny.

Lacy was back at the stairs having explored the whole floor without having caught sight of Joansie, Harley, or Evelyn. "Where'd you guys go?" She moved down the stairs so she could see part of the first floor. They weren't there either. She leaned against the wall. This was why she hadn't wanted to split up.

Turning back to the second floor, Lacy stopped short of running into Harley. "Harley," she gasped placing a hand over her racing heart, "why didn't you say something?"

Harley just smiled.

"Where's Joansie?" Lacy peered around Harley, wondering where the other girl had gotten to.

"I thought she was with you," Harley said, a confused look crossing her face.

"No, you guys left me when we came up the stairs."

Harley smiled slightly. "That was just a little joke. I thought it would be funny."

"Well, it wasn't. And now Joansie's missing too." Lacy walked back down the stairs, uncomfortable with how closely Harley followed. "Why would you do something like that?"

She caught Harley's shrug from the corner of her eye.

"So where is Joansie?" Harley was acting strange. Maybe she

didn't know what to say.

"I don't know. Did you see any sign of her up there?"

"No, I didn't see her. Did you see any signs of Evelyn?"

"No, no signs of Evelyn either. I highly doubt she would have come here, but we needed to look anyway."

"Now we need to search for Joansie too."

"She'll catch up to us eventually. Let's keep looking for Evelyn. She's the one that has me worried. A joke wouldn't have lasted this long."

Lacy agreed. "Stay with me this time, ok? I don't think it's a good idea for any of us to be left alone."

"Alright." Harley said from right behind her, making her jump. "I'll stick with you. And when we find Joansie, she'll stick with us too."

"Good."

Lacy paced outside the antique store. Nowhere. They were nowhere to be found. Worriedly, she chewed at her thumbnail. Jerking her hand away from her mouth, Lacy stared at her thumb in confusion. She'd broken that habit years ago. This was making her crazy.

Lacy looked at Harley. "Nothing?"

Harley didn't say anything but the look in her eyes gave the information away.

"She's not in there?"

Shaking her head, Harley looked at the ground. "I couldn't find her anywhere. Maybe she went out the back door when she first hid and couldn't hear us calling for her."

Throwing up her hands, Lacy turned sharply away from Harley to keep from hitting her. This was exactly why she hadn't wanted to split up in the first place. They were wasting time, fooling around, while Evelyn was missing.

"I guess we'll just have to go around back to look for her."

"I'm really sorry about this." Harley shifted from foot to foot, twisting her hands together.

"Whatever." Lacy didn't want apologies. "Let's just find her so we can find Evelyn and get out of here."

She headed around the side of the building, avoiding inside the claustrophobia-inducing shop. Lacy could hear Harley's quiet steps following behind. Coming around the corner, she found the backyard unimpressive. And empty. Not a surprise. Something would have gone right this trip if Joansie was back there.

Lacy went to the back door to find it locked. "What?" She tried twisting the handle again.

"Maybe it locks automatically, like some office doors do." A shiver ran down her spine at the sound of Harley so close behind her.

Looking over her shoulder, she peered at Harley trying to determine if she was joking.

"I'm serious," Harley read Lacy's expression accurately. "It would need to open easily from inside but be secure against thieves."

"We're out in the middle of nowhere." Lacy gestured to the small corpse of trees beyond the cleared space. "What thieves are they protecting against?"

"This isn't the height of tourist season, Lacy." Harley's voice rose at the way Lacy kept questioning her.

"It was just a suggestion."

Harley shrugged, bringing her anger under control.

Taking a deep breath, Lacy nodded. She was anxious to find the others and get out of there. This little town gave her the creeps.

"Look." Lacy pointed to a path leading into the woods. "Do you think she would hide out in there?" Lacy thought it sounded ridiculous, but Joansie was known to do things boarding on the ridiculous just for the shock. Hiding in the woods while they were looking for Evelyn was possibly something she would do.

Harley shrugged.

"Does that sound like something she would do right now?" Lacy tried to keep her voice level and calm. It would be useless to get angry at Harley. All it would do was cause more friction and slow down their search for their friends.

"She could have." Harley shrugged again. "I'm not sure, but she likes making waves like that."

Sighing, Lacy nodded and set out down the path, determined to find Evelyn and Joansie. The woods were a stupid place to hide, especially in a place they were unfamiliar with.

Lacy heard Harley behind her as they both walked quietly down the path. The trees loomed over them, branches empty of leaves, creating a feeling of walking in a different place and time. Lacy shivered, overcome by a feeling of dread. Harley walked so close to Lacy it was starting to make her uncomfortable. The bare trees surrounding them cast sinister shadows they had to travel through.

Lacy shivered, holding her arms tight across her chest. She felt as if she was walking to her doom.

"How far do you think Joansie went?"

When Lacy didn't get an answer, she paused to look over her shoulder at Harley. Before she could see her, Harley pushed hard on her back, making her stumble forward.

"What…" Lacy gasped, shocked by Harley's action.

Harley pushed her again, harder, almost making her fall.

"Harley, what are you doing?" Lacy took a couple of quick steps away, keeping Harley from pushing her again, before turning to look at her.

Harley's face was impassive as she stared at Lacy. She took a couple of steps toward her with Lacy mirroring those steps to keep the distance between them. Without speaking, she contin-ued taking steps a few at a time, forcing Lacy to move farther into the woods.

"Why are you acting this way?" A quick glance over her shoulder verified there was nothing behind her.

"What way?" Lacy shivered at Harley's bland tone. She spoke as if this was just another day, and they were out for a leisurely walk. What was going on?

"You're acting strange, Harley. What is going on with you? Where are the others?"

Lacy had a feeling Harley knew exactly where the other girls were. She was behind the reason why they were missing, and now Lacy was alone with her. Had she ever really known Harley?

Harley smirked, ignoring Lacy's first questions. "You'll see Joansie and Evelyn soon. Keep walking."

Lacy shook her head, refusing to go any farther. She was cra-zy.

"Move!" Harley shouted, making Lacy jump away from her and deeper into the woods.

They weren't going to get anywhere with a standoff, so Lacy moved down the path. There was no reasoning with crazy, and Harley was certifiable.

The path ended at a clearing, filled with two tied-up girls on their knees. It also contained a long stone slab set on what looked like a boulder at the far end.

Joansie didn't look any different, but Evelyn's eyes were wild. Lacy ran to her, fumbling at the ties around her wrists. Before she could untie them, she was forcefully pulled away, thrown to the ground, and landed on her butt.

Scrambling to her feet, Lacy turned to face Harley. She wasn't going to say anything this time. It wasn't like Harley answered her anyway.

"You will bring us prosperity for the next seven years." When Harley raised her hands at her sides, palms up, a group of cloaked figures emerged from the trees. "You should be honored."

"Honored?" Lacy echoed incredulously.

"Yes, honored. We don't just choose anybody."

Lacy stopped listening, her attention on the altar at the other end of the clearing. Having read about them, she never thought to see one in person. Looking around at the figures surrounding them, Lacy shuddered at the thought she had sought their help to find her friends. They had known where they were this whole time.

Two of them went to Joansie, taking her by her arms and leading her to the altar. Lacy couldn't believe Joansie went quietly with them. She wondered if Harley dosed her with something to keep her calm.

Watching the cloaked figures, Lacy saw they all were focused on what was happening with Joansie. Slowly, she made her way to Evelyn's side. Nobody seemed to notice her move. Harley glanced at her once but made no comment. Lacy thought it was because she didn't think Lacy had the guts to do anything.

She thought wrong.

Lacy looked at Joansie, seeing four figures stripping her. They worked methodically, making her wonder if it was part of their ritual. Not that she cared, if it kept their attention away from her.

Kneeling, Lacy blocked Evelyn's hands from view with her body, hoping nobody saw what she was doing.

"Stay still." Lacy murmured to Evelyn, trying to calm her. "We need to wait for the right moment before making a run for it."

Lacy wasn't sure Evelyn even understood what she was telling her, but she didn't stop. Hoping it looked like she was comforting Evelyn, Lacy kept working on the ties binding her.

"They're all focused on Joansie. We need to make sure we don't do anything to draw their attention. Don't make any sudden movements after I get you free."

Holding her breath, Lacy drew away the ties, freeing Evelyn, praying she wouldn't do anything rash. Evelyn didn't move, still showing no signs she heard her.

Joansie's sharp, short scream jerked their attention to her. Lacy choked back a scream, not believing what she saw.

Joansie lay stretched out on the alter, her limbs twitching and jerking within the grasp of the four people holding her down. Lacy blinked, trying to erase the image of an ornate knife handle sticking out of her chest. She would see that in her nightmares for the rest of her life.

Evelyn screamed, having got to her feet while Lacy was transfixed by the events unfolding before her. She screamed again, breaking into a run heading deeper into the woods. Lacy reached out to her, wanting to stop her and knowing she was too late. There was no way she could catch up to her without being caught herself.

Seeing three of the remaining figures chase after Evelyn, Lacy realized it left only one other person besides Harley. Now was her chance.

Not willing to give up, Lacy sprinted back the way they had come. Toward town. And the car. She could hear the sounds of pursuit but wouldn't risk looking back to see how close they were.

Lacy had taken up running for exercise in between college courses, which helped in her mad dash for freedom. She didn't know how far ahead of them she was when she broke through the trees into the manicured back lawns of the businesses and homes at the edge of town, and she wasn't waiting around to find out.

Lacy didn't stop running until she reached the car. Her hands trembled so badly she could barely hold the hide-a-key box. She dropped it twice before retrieving the key hidden within.

Her chest heaving, Lacy tried to keep her panic from overwhelming her.

Joansie was dead.

Evelyn was lost and as good as dead.

Harley was crazy and had led them all to the quaint little town where the people wanted to kill them.

Trying to breathe deep through her nose so she wouldn't hyperventilate, Lacy dove into the driver's seat, slamming and locking the door behind her. At the end of the street, Lacy saw Harley standing next to a tall woman, panting.

They saw her at the same time, breaking into a run, trying to intercept her.

Thrusting the key into the ignition, Lacy turned it hard, causing the car to start with a growl. Throwing it into drive, the tires squealed as Lacy pressed the gas pedal to the floor. She fishtailed out of the parking lot. Harley had the other set of keys, so letting her get close was out of the question. Locked doors were no deterrent.

Speeding out the other end of town, Lacy had no time to avoid the body that came hurdling out of the woods into the middle of the road. It bounced off the bumper, spinning into the gutter on the side. She couldn't even tell if it had been a man or a woman.

Lacy didn't stop, her bloodless fingers gripping the wheel.

She couldn't stop.

She drove through the night, refusing to look back. Every time she looked in the rearview mirror, she saw Joansie staring back at her with accusing eyes crying tears of blood.

This was one road trip Lacy would never forget.

Beyond the Nebulous Void

Daniel Yocom

A bead of perspiration tickled Mike's ribs as he sat. He knew he was being scryed. Why else would they make him wait in an uncomfortable plastic molded chair to defend his paper to the Journal of Magical Engineering? But this was his opportunity to advance his career beyond the confines of a lower-class space freighter's engine room.

Mike's insides were twisted into a knot. A slithering, tangled mess, like one of those snake balls he had read about.

The secretary looked like an undergrad working for the tuition reduction, who brought him to the waiting area approached from down the hall. Mike reached down and unplugged his tablet from the wall and stuffed the device and cord into his leather bag. It was fully charged before he arrived on campus, but he didn't want any unexpected problems.

She opened the door to the adjoining conference room and waited for Mike. "They're ready for you now, Mr. Carroll."

Mike stood, adjusted his tie and robe, took a deep breath, picked up his bag, and entered.

A large wood table confronted him. Windows along the opposite wall looked down on the central quad. At the far end of the table sat two wizards and an empty chair the secretary filled.

At this end of the room, a single chair waited expectantly. The slithering feelings inside Mike urged him to make a run for the closing door. The quivering in his knees pushed him to sit. He carefully placed his tablet on the table.

Mike recognized the dean, O'Malley. The wizard's picture was in better condition than the man. O'Malley's beard was lopsided, most of his left eyebrow was missing, and that side of his face had a red hue. "Have a seat, young man. We have some questions for you about the paper you submitted to the Journal of Magical Engineering."

The dean's voice was calm but intense, "You don't look like you could grow a beard, yet you claim to be a full Magical Engineer on the starship Nebulas Void?"

"Yes, sir. I—"

"How can this be? You're required to have a bachelor's degree and five years as an Associate before you can take the exams for Engineer. If a Senior Engineer put you up to this, you'll both be presented for review by a guild tribunal."

Mike shifted in his seat. "Sir. I started my university studies before graduating high school and gained my degree when I was eighteen. I passed the Engineer exams three months ago. The paper I submitted was my own work." This wasn't the first time someone questioned his ability based on his age. "If you would like me to demonstrate my spell capabilities, I can."

The dean scrunched his forehead and glared down the table at Mike. He was sure it was meant to look intimidating, but at this distance, with a missing eyebrow, it was more comical than serious. Dean O'Malley glanced at the wizard sitting next to him. She looked down the table at Mike, and he could feel her gaze attempting to pierce his thoughts. The secretary typed on her tablet.

"That isn't required." The dean leaned back and steepled his fingers in front of him. His voice went low and calm. "The first question: how did someone without an advanced degree, or the experience to be a Senior Magical Engineer, even start to link together the underpinnings of the theoretical intertwining of Kepler's Astrological Configuration, Newton's Magic Mass in Motion, Randall's Particle Entanglement, with Ubad's Propulsion Theorem?"

The snakes in Mike's gut were untwining and beginning to hiss at the insults of his age and experience.

He took a slow breath and allowed the silence to hang in the room. "It is true I do not have an advanced degree. My situation in life required me to take employment after earning my bachelor's. My desire to know magic and in particular magical engineering were aroused at a young age. I completed almost two years of core curriculum by the time I graduated from public schools at age sixteen. That allowed me to take upper division courses of engineering, and—"

"We don't want a history lesson." The dean's words carried a vibration through the table though they were whispered. "Just answer the question: what prompted you to start contemplating advanced rune manipulation?"

"Space travel on a third-class freighter with a limited crew is boring and tedious."

The dean either raised his left eyebrow or squinted his right eye. Again, Mike thought he was trying to look imposing. The other wizard quickly covered her mouth and gave an awkward cough. Her eyes were darting back and forth between Mike and the dean.

Mike's snakes turned on each other. He felt the dead and dying piling up in the lower levels of his abdomen. Under his robe, his shirt stuck to his skin. He visually measured the distance to the door while the recycled air got harder to breathe.

"So, you think you can take shortcuts? Bypass the codes of the guild leadership and create a whole new system of crystal confinement because you think space travel is boring?"

"No, sir. There is little to do on the Void—it's aptly named. Our Senior Engineer is a good person but doesn't want to talk to any of the rest of us magicians on board unless the power matrix or containment crystals are having problems. Those systems are well established, and in the three years I've been employed on the Nebulas Void, there hasn't been any issue needing his involvement. I think that's why he's been Senior Engineer for so long on that ship."

Mike stopped. No one moved or spoke. The muscles in his legs tightened, and his knee started bouncing. He couldn't run away so he dove deeper.

He lifted his tablet. "I couldn't afford to return to school. Instead, I loaded every text and research book I could find from every outpost we've traveled to since I took the assignment. I've spent my spare time with the great magicians of history. Copernicus, Galileo, Randall, and others have been my Senior Engineers. I've read what I could and then started working on new possibilities. I didn't put anything into practice. I would never jeopardize a crew or a ship."

"Well, since you didn't destroy the ship, yourself, or everyone else on board, you might have some of the intelligence that shows in your submission."

Mike didn't see where the old wizard had produced the notebook he was now holding, but he knew it was his journal submission. O'Malley opened the binder and leafed through the pages.

"You're telling us that you never thought about putting these runes onto a containment crystal?"

"I thought about it." The dean's head snapped up. "But I never did it. For two reasons: I can't afford to buy or make my own crystals, and I am not going to risk an inner-dimensional pocket on an operating starship, no matter how bored I get."

The glare didn't go away as the dean closed the folder. "Your conclusions are flawed. You would have created just such a pocket."

The snakes stopped moving. They slumped and fell into a cold lump in the bottom of his gut. "In that case, I will withdraw my paper for consideration in the journal. I will continue my personal studies, and when I feel I have something worthy enough for consideration by this esteemed body of collegiate individuals, I will submit it then." Mike put his hands on the edge of the table and pushed his chair back.

"We're not done, Mr. Carroll, and you haven't been excused."

"Sir, you are saying my theory is inaccurate. I believe you have already told me this paper is not worthy of publication. What more needs to be discussed?"

"Sit down. You may have developed a decent understanding of the dead magicians of history and their theories, but it is perilously obvious you don't spend very much time with the living, magician or not. Do you think you were invited here to defend your submission to a journal? If that was all, we would've sent you a rejection letter like we do with everyone else. We have busy schedules. I wanted to see the person who wrote this. I wanted to find out what would drive a person to work on this level of theoretical possibilities without being here under these roofs."

Mike slumped in the chair.

"Furthermore, everything I've asked so far, I could've got without you being present. Now, close your mouth before you start drooling like the fool you almost showed yourself to be. Thank you."

O'Malley stood, and Mike felt very small. "Mr. Carroll, there is more at stake here. More than you apparently understand. This was to see what type of drive you have—what you have on the inside besides a brain. Your paper shows you have one of those. It just needs some rough edges knocked off."

The dean looked again at the wizard at his end of the table, and she nodded. The secretary typed.

"We wanted to know if you could handle yourself under pressure. See what you would do."

"I don't understand."

"Of course, you don't. You weren't meant to understand you were coming to an interview because you would've declined. Do you think we didn't check you out before we sent an invitation to defend your paper? Of course, we did. Of course, we know your background. I even talked to some of your professors. Even though it has been five years since you attended school, almost every one of them remembered you. One even asked if I was there because of some honor to be bestowed upon you as you were being elevated to a post doctorate position. They have high hopes for you, Mr. Carroll."

Mike worked at forming a question. Nothing came. He could only look at the other people in the room.

"Final question for you, Mr. Carroll. Do you want to continue your education here at the University?"

"I can't afford it."

"That wasn't the question."

"Want, yes. That's what I've always wanted."

The old wizard looked over at the woman who had covered her mouth. Dean O'Malley pointed with his hand toward her as he looked back at Mike. "This is Professor Hawke. She is one of our best in the School of Engineering. She is also the current editor of the Journal of Magical Engineering. And she is the one who brought me your paper. I, in turn, verified past academic record and employment history."

The dean watched Mike, nodding slightly. "Yes, I think the light is starting to come on inside that skull of yours. So please, close your mouth again. Thank you. You are being offered a stipend to match your current salary so you can take care of your parents' needs. For that stipend, you will be working with Professor Hawke. She has been working the past few years along similar lines to what you have been doing on your own. She has, in fact, created one of those inner-dimensional pockets. Which was thankfully contained in a fully functional laboratory." He sat back down with his hand on his chest, shaking his head.

"At least, young man, you were smart enough not to attempt such an experiment on a starship. If you had, you probably wouldn't be here to give us a decision of joining our doctorate program or going back to the boring confines of a ship that is so horribly named as the Nebulas Void."

They clearly have planned something. Dr. Hawke watched the dean, while still looking at Mike. He made sure he didn't allow his mouth to open.

"Well, Dr. Hawke?"

She spoke one clear word as she nodded. "Yes."

Perotine

Emmeline de Vere

"**M**adame Massey, do you recognize this goblet?"

Perotine took a deep breath as she looked at the ornate silver cup in the Bailiff's hand, giving herself time to carefully choose her words. Her fingers squeezed and rubbed at her pale blue skirts, though none of the onlookers could see that through the ornately carved oak of the witness stand. Like many things on the island of Guernsey, the courtroom was as ambitious and self-important as it was small. A dozen onlookers crowded the gallery opposite the stand where she stood, curious neighbors and officious priests among them. They shifted and tugged at their collars in the July heat, making Perotine wonder if they regretted their decision to gawk at her trial today.

Even as she participated in them, Perotine watched the proceedings with the same curiosity that had marked the twenty years of her life so far. As a child, it made her ask how hedgehogs made babies without getting prickled. Two years ago, when she met a Calvinist man recently arrived from France, it made her fascinated enough with his radical ideas that she became his wife. And one night last year when she was out fetching water and saw a dancing light in the distance that seemed to speak directly into her mind, her curiosity compelled her follow to where the wisp led. Now it made her wonder why the questioning focused so much more on her than on her mother and sister. She would be lucky if the questions ventured no more widely than stolen goblets.

"Yes, Monsieur, I recognized it as stolen from Nicholas le Conronney, when Mademoiselle Gosset offered it to me in exchange for lending her sixpence. I gave her the money, but only so she would not give the goblet to anyone else. I shared my suspicions with Monsieur le Conronney that same day."

"Please answer only the questions you are asked, Madame Massey."

Perotine stiffened and clenched her jaw. It was bad enough having her life in the hands of a Jerseyman. Having it in the hands of a smug and money-grubbing man like Helier Gosselin was intolerable.

"I do recognize it."

"And do you deny that you, your mother, or sister solicited Mademoiselle Gosset to steal it for you?"

"I do deny it."

"Thank you, Madame. That will be all."

Already?

Perotine cradled her pregnant belly as she slowly turned to leave the stand. She should have been relieved that he'd not asked about the timing of her husband's departure and the growing child in her womb, or her frequenting of ancient dolmens in the dead of night. Instead, the Bailiff's focus on the trivially false allegation of the stolen goblet suggested that the questions did not matter at all. The smug smile from the Dean in the gallery only magnified that suspicion.

"Monsieur Thomas Effart will please take the stand."

Perhaps Perotine's neighbor would have put on his Sunday best when summoned to court as a young man, but he certainly did not now. Monsieur Effart wore the same brown woolen trousers as when he tended his garden, and he shambled to the stand with the same deliberate pace. The wisps of stark white hair on his head seemed even more thin than Perotine remembered. His grip on the witness stand's rail was even more skeletal.

"Monsieur Effart, the Bailiwick is grateful for your service at court today," the Bailiff began, "I promise my questions will be few. Would you please tell the court how long you have known Madame Massey and her family?"

Monsieur Effart smacked his lips before speaking. "Oh… I've lived next to the mother Catherine for at least thirty years. Well before the girls were born."

The Bailiff nodded, unsurprised. "Today, Madame Massey stands accused of suborning the theft of a silver goblet by Mademoiselle Virginie Gosset. Tell me Monsieur Effart, are you familiar with Mademoiselle Gosset?"

"I could not say that I know her well. Only that I have heard her name in relation to some of the roughs in town."

The Bailiff nodded again, impatiently this time. "And would the theft described here today be in keeping with the character of Madame Massey and her family?"

"In the decades they've lived next to my farm, I have never known Madame Cauchés or her daughters to be thieves," Monsieur Effart replied. "Quite the contrary, they have many times helped to return my cows when they escape my fields. In recent years they've also patched my pasture walls. The stones are so much heavier than they used to be."

The audience laughed at Monsieur Effart's self-effacing humor, and Perotine smiled in gratitude. At least he was on their side.

The Bailiff was less pleased. He leaned in closer, staring into Monsieur Effart's eyes.

"Then they are of perfect moral character, not a fault to be found?"

The witness scowled back the Bailiff indignantly. "They are as good of people as you'll find on this island, with not a fault larger than missing Mass on a Sunday."

The Bailiff paused a moment, before his lips slowly curled to a grin.

"Thank you Monsieur Effart, that will be all." The Bailiff's grin remained as he watched Perotine's old neighbor slowly return to the gallery. His eyes flicked to the Catholic Dean, who returned his smile with a nod.

"In the matter of Monsieur le Conronney's stolen goblet," the Bailiff addressed the court, "I find Virginie Gosset guilty of theft and perjury. She is to have her ear nailed to a pillory in the town square. I find Catherine Cauchés and her daughters Perotine and Guillemine to be innocent, and they are acquitted of all charges."

Perotine closed her eyes as she sighed with relief. *Thank God.*

She felt her mother squeeze her hand.

"Your Excellency," said a male voice from the gallery. "If I may?"

What now? Perotine opened her eyes. The Dean stood in the gallery, slender almost to the point of gauntness, yet commanding the attention of the room despite his slight frame. His high-collared cassock was unadorned, but its silken shine still showed him a stranger to poverty or toil. Perotine guessed him to be nearly fifty, with spots of grey speckling the dark brown hair beneath his skullcap. He looked at the Bailiff expectantly.

"The court recognizes Dean Jaques Amy. What is your request, Master Dean?" The Bailiff answered quickly and smoothly, as though expecting the Dean's question.

"Though your Excellency has doubtless exercised perfect justice today under the laws of our Bailiwick, the testimony has uncovered even more grave transgressions of the laws of our god and monarch. The spurning of the ordinances of the church is a sign of rebellion that should not pass without further scrutiny.

I request that the accused be secured in Castle Cornet while I conduct an examination of the depth of their heresy."

The Bailiff made a show of deliberating on the request, stroking his short beard as he looked from the Dean to Perotine. A knot of fear tightened in her stomach. She wondered if the baby could feel it.

"The petition of the church is granted. The accused will be remanded to the castle for examination."

Perotine's fear turned to numbness when the guards prodded the three women out of the court and forced them into the back of an open wagon to be taken to the castle. For once, she did not notice the jostling of the wheels on the cobbled streets, or the beauty of the harbor below as they made the short descent into St. Pierre Port. As she was escorted into the castle by the guards, her fear warred with her curiosity. What reason could there be for these rulers of the island to take such an interest in her and her family? Could there be any, other than the strange man she'd met that night fetching water?

"The Dean says this one goes in alone," a guard said, before another pushed her into a stone-walled room barely as wide as she was tall. A tiny slit near the top of the far wall admitted the room's only light. The guard closed the heavy wooden door behind her, and she heard the heavy clank of iron as the lock's bolt slid home.

The room was silent and mostly empty. A small pile of straw in one corner passed for furnishings, likely already sheltering some kind of vermin. Perotine stood silently, resting her forehead on the cold stone wall, taking shaky, measured breaths as she tried to hold back tears of frustration and despair. If only she could hear their actual charges instead of puffed-up pretenses. If only she could have a chance to defend herself. If only he was here. The weight of her pregnant belly pressed on her feet and bent her back until she finally conceded and sat on the straw in her skirts, vermin be damned.

It seemed like hours before she heard the lock turn again, though by the light from the slit, it could not have been many. The door creaked as Perotine looked up and saw the guard push it open and the Dean enter, still in his fine black cassock.

"How uncivilized," said the Dean with mock outrage. "You have the lady on the floor, and in her condition. Fetch us two chairs and leave us be."

The Dean stepped close and extended his hand to help her up. She stared at it, outraged at the show of manners while he so casually toyed with her family's lives. She hated herself for taking his hand in hers to help her stand. The guard returned with two battered wooden chairs, likely taken from the guards themselves, and left her alone with the Dean.

"Ma petite sorchiére, please, take a seat. I am so happy we finally have this chance to talk. You have no idea the amount of attention you have received of late."

Sorchiére? How much did he know? How could he have known? They had been so careful. She needed to be careful still.

"What are you talking about? What man accuses me of withering his cattle or shriveling his loins? There is none."

The Dean shook his head slowly, ignoring his own chair as he paced, like a teacher exasperated with a slow learning student. "Ma petite désourcheul'raesse, then. Black witch or white, it makes no difference." He gestured to where her round belly made her high-waisted skirt arch out in front of her as he continued pacing in circles around her chair. "This. This is the problem. Your husband fled last October, yet here it is July and the time of your travail is not yet arrived. Anyone with all their fingers could guess who the father is not. I know as well as you who he actually is

163

"But in truth, it is not even about you, Madame," the Dean continued. "Did your fallen lover not tell you why this place is special? Did you not wonder how he found you here? This island sits not just close to France, but close to the border between our world and his. It is too strategic, too close to the other side to be ruled by Aza's bastard. Seigneur Azael will keep it for his own."

"You…" she began, her thoughts coming faster than her words could keep up, "…a sorchier devoted to Azael." The Dean was driven not by Catholic zeal, but loyalty to his own fallen master. He knew about her child's father. He knew more about the other side than she, most likely. *Does he know everything?* He could not know of the understanding with her husband, how she kept his secret in exchange for him keeping hers. He could not know how Aza twined freesias into her hair and called her "my flower".

The Dean laughed softly, reaching down to brush back a dark lock of her hair and stroke her cheek with the back of his fingers. "I see you begin to understand. It's a pity you chose sides so poorly. Let me guess, Aza promised you knowledge. Even shared some. He taught you of plants and cures. He taught you the arts of pleasure and lovemaking. He promised you ascension to the stars by the ineffable name. Yet, here you sit."

The accuracy of the Dean's guesses pierced her heart to the core. She could not let that show.

"Nothing I say can save me, can it? We were dead the moment we were arrested."

"Almost. The Gosset girl bungled things hopelessly, but Monsieur Effart gave me all I needed in the end."

The dear fool.

"Really you should be grateful to him. Heretics are merely burned. To try you as a witch we'd have to strip your clothes…"

He paused as he tugged at the neckline of her dress, exposing more of her shoulder and chest.

"…shave every hair from your body…"

He trailed his fingertips over her skin, his soft priest's hands even less calloused than hers. Perotine balled her fists in her skirt, struggling to remain still.

"…and examine and prick every inch of you to find your witch's mark."

Two fingers made sharp, walking jabs down the bare top of her breast, punctuating his words.

Perotine swatted away his hand, shivering as she stared indignantly up at him. She leaned as far from him as she could in the small chair until it threatened to tip.

"This is no mercy," she spat back at him. "A witch hunt could draw attention to your own allegiance. You charge heresy instead because it keeps you safe."

The Dean laughed, conceding the point as he withdrew his hand. "Even so, the result is the same."

"I plead the belly." Perotine's hands returned to cradle her roundness. "You cannot execute a woman who is with child."

The Dean shook his head. "You can raise that with the Bailiff, Madame, but old custom will not save you. Queen Mary has again aligned the crown with the church and scours the land for heretics. I could execute the Bailiff himself if I wished."

Perotine closed her eyes and breathed, thinking, trying to find some other exit from her plight. She found none.

Aza, where are you?

Perotine opened her eyes and looked back at the Dean coldly. "Then why are we here? Why reveal all this, or torment me with false hope?"

The Dean finally took his seat in the chair opposite her. "Oh, it wouldn't do to rush things, would it? We both know the importance of keeping up appearances. It takes time for me to examine your faith and give you every opportunity to renounce your Calvinist heresies. Just as it takes time for you to reaffirm them and make shocking slanders of our Queen. We must be seen to be thorough."

Aza, please! she cried in her mind, hoping he would sense her desperation. Only silence answered her. He would not know of her plight until she failed to appear that evening.

"You are a monster. You defile the sanctity of your office."

"Oh, do not pretend to find my office sacred. As a Calvinist and a witch, you are doubly a heretic. It is deliciously ironic, though, is it not? Aza's consort being put to death not for her witchcraft, but for her Calvinism."

Three sharp knocks on the door interrupted the Dean's taunting.

"Open," said the Dean loudly.

The bolt slid back, and the door swung in, revealing the same guard from before.

"Master Dean, the Bailiff has returned to hear your report."

"Just in time," he replied, "though I fear the only hope of redemption for these three is to be found in the flames. This one," he pointed to Perotine, "in particular. Gag her and bring them all above."

The guard hesitated, his eyes taking in Perotine's obviously pregnant figure.

"Do your duty," the Dean ordered. "Or do you share her heretical sympathies?"

"No, my lord, er, Master Dean."

Perotine tried to resist the rope he pressed between her lips, holding her teeth tightly closed and thrashing her head side to side. It was futile. The guard pulled on the rope behind her head and drew it taut, finally getting it between her teeth when she involuntarily cried out. He bound her hands then prodded her back out the narrow passages of the stone keep where the Dean had gone.

The Dean was already speaking to the Bailiff when she emerged. She caught only the end of his report, as her mother and sister were brought out behind her, but it was enough.

"...no hope for them but absolution and purification in the holy flames, I fear. This one in particular," the Dean gestured at Perotine, "had to be gagged to end her gross imprecations against our God and Queen and to prevent her falling even deeper into sin."

For once the Bailiff seemed unsure, looking from the Dean to Perotine and back, as though he only just realized he was about to execute three innocent women, one of them pregnant. He stepped close to the Dean and spoke quietly.

"Master Dean, are you quite sure?"

"Her Majesty has made the punishment for heresy quite clear, your Excellency. Heretics are to be burned, and their property reverted to the crown. Of course, that would place the burden of handling their property upon yourself." The Dean gave the Bailiff an unbroken stare as the half-spoken bribe hung in the air.

The Bailiff considered for a moment, his eyes flickering one more time to the women and back, before he spoke to the guard.

"For heresy against God and insubordination against the Queen, the accused are sentenced to be stripped and burnt at the stake until their bones become ash."

Perotine heard her mother and sister cry out in anguish. They had not been gagged as she had. *They do not deserve this.* They were as Calvinist as she was, but had no knowledge of Perotine's liaisons with Aza or the Dean's secret motives. She gnawed futilely against the rope gagging her mouth, feeling her own saliva seep into the fibers and moisten her cheeks.

The Dean glanced at Perotine, smiling contentedly.

"As you command, your Excellency," the guard replied. "Any retentum?"

The Bailiff looked again at Perotine, his head tilted to the side in thought. "Have them strangled at the stake before the burning. Let no man say I am without mercy."

The guards and Bailiff wasted no time in carrying out the sentence.

Perotine felt an unexpected calm when the guards led her down the castle causeway to town, while her mother and sister pleaded and struggled. Unlike them, she needed no prodding. She climbed the granite steps of Tower Hill in a daze, numb to the exertion even in her pregnant state.

She was jarred from her trance by the sound of ripping cloth and the cool of the sea breeze against the skin of her back. A guard with a knife had sliced the fabric of her dress down the back then began to cut through the sleeves. She almost laughed at how delicately he sliced the dress away, carefully avoiding any damage to her skin even as he prepared her for execution.

Seigneur Azael will have an unblemished lamb for his sacrifice.

Other guards erected three posts next to the green in the center of the square, fumbling to brace them upright and shouting at each other to find more firewood. They were not well practiced at burning heretics.

Two guards prodded her mother and sister toward the stands. They were as nude as she was. Perotine looked away. Seeing them naked and humiliated wrenched at her heart in a way that their cries had not. She could reduce their shame by one pair of eyes, at least.

She looked down instead. Her round belly obscured her view of her own feet. Its smooth skin was interrupted by the dark line that had appeared in the fourth month of her pregnancy, and the navel that had begun to protrude in her fifth. Her fretting over those changes seemed so trivial now. She saw her breasts, full and heavy where they had once sat high and pointed, her nipples so much darker than she remembered. Her son would never suckle there.

My son.

Aza had told her it would be a boy. She had learned not to question how he knew what he did. He would teach her in time.

We had so much less time than we thought.

The guards came for her now, leading her to the third, unoccupied post. As she turned, she noticed an ache in her lower abdomen and back. Her first step triggered a cramp in her core that was a dozen times more painful than her monthly courses. She doubled over, unable to catch herself, and felt the cobbles slam into her shoulder and side. She cried as the guard tried to lift her, but her legs refused to work for several moments until the pain subsided.

It must have ended, and she must have stood, but she could not remember when or how. Perotine found herself tied to the stake, feet resting on roughly cut firewood. She looked out at the gathering crowd. The Bailiff and Dean were there, watching the guards draw straws. The loser shook his head and left the group, then picked up a truncheon and a short length of cord that had been set on the ground nearby.

He walked toward the women, then past Perotine and out of sight. She heard her mother cry out again, making her last desperate plea in a jumble of English and Guernesiais. The crowd quieted as her mother's words did, replaced by the sound of rope twisting against wood, breathless gurgling, and the slap of limbs flailing against naked flesh. It was not long before the sound stopped altogether.

Tears streamed from Perotine's eyes and down her cheeks, joining her spittle in the rough rope as she heard the guard move from one stake to the other behind her. Where her mother had begged, Perotine's sister merely sobbed. But like her mother, the sound ceased when the cord tightened around her neck. She heard nothing from her sister after that, only knowing that her final moment had passed when the crowd's morbid staring was replaced again by whispered chatter.

This is the Bailiff's mercy.

Perotine did not see the guard approach. She felt his fingers on her shoulder as he passed the cord around her neck, and its tug against her throat as he tied the knot around both her and the post. She felt it suddenly squeeze as he inserted the truncheon into the loop and began to turn, tightening the cord further with each twist. It cut into her, making her gasp, and then preventing even that. The world began to disappear, replaced by black and dancing sparks.

She heard a crack, and the world came rushing back as she desperately wheezed air back into her lungs.

"Aza, thank you," she said aloud, well past the fear of being heard.

She heard a man's voice, but not her lover's.

"The damned rope broke!" the guard shouted back toward the other guards and Bailiff.

It was the Dean's voice that answered. "The Almighty has shown that this heretic's soul must remain to be purified by the flames. Carry on!"

The guards waited, unmoving, until the Bailiff nodded his agreement. One approached with a lit torch, walking past her to start with her mother as the first guard had done. He studiously avoided Perotine's gaze as he passed.

She heard the fire first, after some muttering by the guard. The popping and billowing sounds of a warm hearth on a damp night now promised her death. Then she smelled it, the smoke from the burning fibers and resins of the wood not quite masking the smell of charring flesh. It made her gag. Her body heaved against the bonds that held her fast to the post. Finally, she felt it, first as warmth, then as heat, then as searing pain around her feet and ankles.

It triggered the other pain, deep inside. Another contraction of her womb. Suddenly a gush of wetness flowed out of her and down her thighs. The onlookers gasped.

The baby was coming. Perotine bit and cried against the gag between her teeth, not knowing whether it would be better for the baby to die inside her or out. She moaned through the pain of another cramping contraction and felt the baby shift inside her. As the flames crept higher around her ankles, she realized the bottoms of her feet had no feeling left.

Out, she decided. There was one thing left in the world that she could possibly control. If she could hold on long enough, and usher her baby into the world soon enough, he might yet live. If she could do that one thing, maybe that was mercy enough.

Against every instinct that told her to avoid the pain, Perotine pushed. She stared at the Dean and Bailiff, seeing them only hazily through the smoke and tears. Each contraction came more closely than the one before. She bit hard into the rope, growling through her gag and channeling her pain and rage into the one purpose she had left in life.

She gasped as she felt movement inside her, and new stabs of pain erupted where her thighs met. Some fresh wetness trickled down her legs, and the murmur of the crowd told her it was blood.

One more push.

Perotine slumped low, sliding her back down against the stake and opening her thighs to ease the baby's passage, before giving the last push that she had the strength to make. She pushed against the pain and the impossible tearing tightness until she felt it slacken.

She looked down but she couldn't see. The crowd erupted with shouting.

"A baby!"

"A child born in the flames!"

A man she did not recognize stepped close to the flaming pile, holding a hunter's knife in his hand. New terror coursed through her already-saturated veins as she watched him reach beneath her. When he pulled back, it was with her baby cradled in his arms. The knife had merely cut the cord that bound her to her son.

Her son.

Aza was right.

The unknown man fled the flames with the babe in his arms. Perotine tried to see where he went, but the smoke in her eyes made it impossible. She tried to straighten to get a better view, but her legs refused to obey.

Never mind. She had done it. There was no reason left to fight. The crushing pain inside had ceased. The burning pain in her legs had mostly faded as well. She slumped against the flaming post. She could endure what remained.

Perotine heard her baby cry.

She heard voices arguing, but she struggled to make out the words.

"...cannot execute a babe..."

"What God has decreed...Her Majesty..."

The haze parted again, and another man stepped close. A guard, by the shade of his boots and breeches. He lowered a cloth-wrapped bundle into her lap.

Her baby.

No. Dear God, no! Aza, please!

She wept, though her eyes could no longer make tears. She tried to shift and shield the baby from the worst of the flames, but there was little her body could do even if she'd not been bound.

Then she saw him. A man, in the flames with her, shining even more brightly than they burned. He lifted the crying bundle from her lap and cradled it to his chest, before wrapping them both in a cooling embrace.

"My flower," he wept. "What have they done to you?"

A fresh uproar from the crowd flooded her ears. They could see him too. They did not matter now.

"Aza…" Perotine whispered hoarsely, "…our son."

"He is beautiful. Tell me his name."

Perotine had not thought that far. They had discussed many names, and they all fit more poorly now than they had then. Then she knew.

"Adam." She coughed. "Call him Adam, and raise him to make a new world better than this."

Aza kissed her forehead, his lips cool against her singed skin, as Perotine breathed her last breath.

Afterword

Perotine Massey lived on Guernsey as the wife of a Calvinist minister during the reign of (Bloody) Mary I. While her husband was in London fleeing persecution in 1556, she, her mother, and her sister were acquitted of receiving a stolen silver goblet, but the questioning of their neighbors revealed they had not been attending Catholic Mass. They were burnt at the stake for heresy. There were no recorded allegations of witchcraft or adultery. Perotine gave birth in the flames, and the Bailiff ordered that her newborn son be thrown back in to burn with her. The three women are known today as the Guernsey Martyrs. The truest horrors are born not from demons beyond, but the monsters that we make ourselves when we drink too deep of zealotry.

Draw Your Own Conclusions

Sara Fitzgerald

Juliet bit her lip, entranced by her newest painting. The brilliant blood dripped down the pale victim's face as she lay amid the center of the canvas. Her haunting blue eyes told a horrifying secret.

"Another splendid show, my dear," said Stanley, the older gentleman who owned the upscale art gallery. "You should be proud of yourself."

A chill traveled through her as if black widows sought their next prey within her. She stared at the knife carelessly left behind at the grisly murder scene in her painting.

"The emotion this piece provokes," he said, placing a gentle hand on her shoulder, "it's hard to describe. The rage someone must have to do such an atrocious thing. Can you even imagine?"

Juliet clutched her velvet gown as her pulse quickened. The large grandfather clock ticked loudly, and the pendulum swung back and forth in a strange rhythmic motion, trying to lure her into a false sense of security.

The gallery doors opened, and a rush of cold air assaulted the intimacy between Stanley and her.

Two detectives entered. Mathew, a large, burly man, nudged the other lanky man, Edward. Both men wore cheap suits, stained ties, and scuffed shoes. Both were middle-aged, cynical souls who knew nothing of culture or class. Their eyes narrowed on her.

The acid in her stomach snaked upward. She swallowed the bitterness of the bile and forced herself to relax her hands.

Stanley turned to them. "The gallery is closed. You missed the show, but please come back tomorrow to view Miss Juliet's work. She's exceptional and a rare find in an artist."

The men strode toward them. The burly one flashed a badge. "I think she can spare us a few moments."

Her stomach tightened. These two always had questions about her pieces. That wasn't new, but unfortunately, her painting was not flawless this time.

"Juliet, you are the ta k of the city." The lanky one crossed his arms. "As are your paintings."

"Yes," said his partner, the burly man with a familiar stench on his breath. "What inspires you to paint such unsettling piec-es?"

Stanley rolled his eyes. "Not this nonsense again. Do you real-ly think Miss Juliet murdered this poor woman?"

"The victim looks exactly like the woman in her painting." Edward frowned, studying the piece.

Stanley waved his hand. "Yes, tragic, but you can't honestly think Miss Juliet had anything to do with it."

Mathew watched her intently.

"The woman's photo was all over the news," Mr. Stanley mut-tered. "This is harassment, plain and simple, just like all those other times. Miss Juliet is not a monster, for God's sake."

"Then why does she paint such horrifying scenes?" Edward's jaw twitched. "And always get the details right."

Her hands trembled, but she fought the rising panic swirling within.

"We got her this time." Edward pointed to the careless knife hidden behind the lush blue loveseat. "This wasn't in the media;

she'd have no idea about it unless she were involved."

Mathew's eyes bulged. "We need to get this in evidence right away. Make the call."

Mathew's grin slipped into his grim face as he took out his handcuffs. "Juliet, you have the right to remain silent."

She tried standing, but her knees collapsed. Mathew yanked her up.

"You are making a grave mistake." Stanley's face blanched. "The only thing Miss Juliet is guilty of is having a brilliant imagination."

Mathew pushed her toward the entrance, leading her out into the darkness of the streets.

"I'll call your attorney, my dear," Stanley said. "Everything will be okay. Do not fret."

Sergeant Miller pursed his chapped lips, glaring at his top detectives, Mathew and Edward. "Listen, this is insane. You cannot hold her. Release her at once."

"She's the killer." Mathew leaned on the desk. "It'd be crazy to let her walk."

Sergeant Miller waved his hand. "The evidence tells a different story. She was home on the nights of the murders, holed up in her studio; the security camera shows her sitting at the easel. Plus, staff verified her whereabouts."

"Come on, you know as well as I do that footage can be messed with, and she pays her staff well; they'd lie for her." Edward crossed his arms. "Let's not forget the knife in her painting. We never released that detail to the public or where we found it."

"Lucky guess on her part." Sergeant Miller drummed his large fingers on the desk, sweat gathering on his brow, his cheeks flushed with frustration.

"She's guilty." Mathew banged his hands on the desk. "For

Pete's sake, she was so nervous when we spoke to her, she could barely stand."

Sergeant Miller's eye twitched; his gut must be screaming the same thing, but the old-timer refused to end his career looking like a fool. "Let her go."

"She could have had a partner." Edward yanked his hand through his messy hair.

Sergeant Miller sighed. "We have been over this; she is a recluse and only spends time with the old man at the gallery. Mr. Stanley is hardly capable of murdering anyone. Plus, he had an alibi for every murder."

"His wife." Mathew rolled his eyes.

Sergeant Miller cleared his throat. "On the Clarence murder, Stanley was in Vermont visiting his sister."

"What about one of her staff?" Edward's jaw clenched. "She could have paid them to do it. The ghastly, bloody murders have made her into a sensation."

"The media is making us the running joke in the city for even suspecting her. We look like bloody fools." Sergeant Miller stood, grabbing his jacket. "Focus your attention elsewhere."

"Can we at least run her prints on the knife?" Mathew asked, hopefully.

Sergeant Miller placed his hat firmly on his bald head. "Keep it on the down low. Understood?"

The detectives nodded. Fear twisted with anger pulsed through their veins. Juliet was a coldhearted, ruthless killer, and they'd prove it.

Juliet sat in the interrogation room. She'd been there chained to the metal chair for hours. The burly and lanky detectives claimed they could not reach her attorney or Mr. Stanley.

The hot air suffocated her as a drip of urine ran down her leg.

She squeezed her bladder tighter, refusing to soil herself. She was not an animal.

The walls shrunk, the dull light flickered, and the low humming of the air vent was driving her mad. Damn her ambition. She wouldn't be in this horrible predicament if she had not been desperate to make a name for herself.

None of her beautiful flowers, vivid sunsets, or breathtaking oceans sold, and she wasn't content being a nobody; she craved attention, admiration, and the illusion of notoriety.

It wasn't until the splashes of red and horror soaked her canvases that her signature took off.

The malicious scenes caught the public's attention, but what made her even more of an immense sensation was the real-life murders colliding with her artwork, making her canvases a delicious treat for the hungry, devious minds of the city.

Mathew waltzed in, stuffing his face with a massive sandwich. Mayo dripped down his double chin. "Sorry to keep you waiting."

"Have you reached my attorney?" She gritted her teeth.

"About that," he said with a smug smile. "Looks like he's out of town until Monday. Guess you'll be stuck here."

Edward's lanky, pathetic body pushed open the door.

"Just tell us how your prints got on the knife and who helped you with the murders." Edward sat across from her and pushed a pad of paper and pen toward her. "Better yet, write down your confession, and we can be done with this."

"You must be thirsty, hungry, tired, not to mention need to use the bathroom." Mathew smirked. "Just make us a pretty confession, and you can leave this room; otherwise, it will be a long night or weekend."

"This is against my rights," she muttered, yanking on the cuff that held her.

She glared at the two detectives, imagining what their faces would look like, warped in death, their cheap suits soaked in blood, and their organs sprawled across the room.

"What about the victims' rights?" Mathew took another bite of his sandwich. This time, a slimy piece of lettuce fell out of his mouth.

"You must be a complete psycho to do the dark, twisted things you've done." Edward pushed the pad closer to her. "Write it down."

She laughed. If only they knew the true terror she was capable of. "You want a confession? I'll give you one."

She snatched the pen and quickly began drawing the images in her mind of the burly and lanky detectives.

Edward stood, terror in his dark eyes, as he grabbed his gun from the holster. He pointed it straight at Mathew.

"What the hell are you doing?" his partner stuttered.

She scribbled more details, and the shattering noise of the gun pierced the quiet room. Mathew's guts sprawled out of him; he grabbed his stomach in horror.

"Look at me," Mathew screamed, his dying form slumped against the metal chair.

She scribbled more. This was wicked and fun.

Edward grabbed Mathew and shot him in the throat, blood splattered everywhere as the burly detective choked on his own damn blood. It was perfect.

She drew as she savored the terror in Edward's eyes. "Let's have some more fun, shall we?"

His eyes widened. "What have you done?"

"You're the one holding the gun." She shrugged. "Perhaps you should have given me my attorney sooner."

He lunged for her, knocking her chair over, but she gripped the pen and pad tightly. Her cruel, twisted laughter echoed in the room.

"Almost finished," she said, grinning. "Say hi to your dead partner."

He slowly raised the gun to his head and pulled the trigger; his brains dispersed everywhere, mingled in with the vivid color of his blood. His body crumbled to the floor.

The room looked like a fantastic horror story of guts, gore, and terror.

She ripped the piece of paper off the pad and stuffed it in her mouth and slowly chewed.

Too bad no one would ever see her brilliant masterpiece.

Danielle Harward

"Gretal, a moment please."

I glanced up from the blank page before me, blinking myself out of the spotlight piece I was supposed to be writing. I clutched the quill in my hand. Old copies of the Fairwood Gazette were strewn about on tables, and writers were scribbling away all around me, preparing their articles for the printing press. But my gaze cut across the room to our editor and chief.

Red gestured to her office as I met her bright gaze before she disappeared back inside it.

Across from me, Stiltskin raised a bushy brow, pausing from writing his classified. The corner of his mouth pulled up into a smirk. Mocking me as if I had just gotten called to the stocks as he picked up golden string and twirled it between his fingers.

I frowned at him, in no mood for his needling. I grabbed my notebook and slipped from my desk.

We, the Fairwood Gazette, existed in a small, dust-covered office smelling of ink and paper. We reported the stories they don't tell you once someone has found their "happily ever after." As if our lives suddenly stopped simply because we achieved a goal. But that is never the case, our lives don't stop, mine certainly didn't after my brother and I escaped the terrifying witch in the woods. I might still gag anytime I saw a piece of candy, but now I was a journalist at one of the most respected newspapers in the kingdom of Fairwood.

I stepped into Red's office, my cheeks instantly flushed from the heat as a fire roared in the ancient stone fireplace next to her desk. Even though it was the middle of summer, our office was cool, and Red liked it warm. Some whispered she was cold blooded and only came alive when she had a heat source nearby, but I suspected it kept nightmares of wolves and cold forests away. We had both been to hell and back at a young age. We lived nightmares. And I suspected that's why she removed the candy bowl from her desk as I took a seat in the cushioned chair.

Red wore her typical black pantsuit, her scarlet hair bright against the stark darkness. She sat at the large wooden desk in the center of the room, scribbling in a notebook. I eyed her knick-knack-and-paper-filled office as I waited. I knew better than to interrupt a writer while they were in the middle of a stream of consciousness.

Without glancing up at me, she asked, "You completed the Cinderella interview?"

My brows furrowed; the deadline wasn't till Friday. Did she know I hadn't started writing it yet? "Has the deadline changed?"

Red stopped writing, glancing up at me. Fire beyond the one next to us shone in her bright green eyes. "Have you finished a first draft?"

I flushed, now beyond the heat in the room. Admittedly, I had not written that story. I hadn't even been able to get a word of an outline on the paper yet. Journalism demands I tell the story without inserting my filter; Red is always pushing that on us writers. We are expected to state facts and report the truth. I thought when I was assigned report on Cinderella's life now that she was Queen in a "where is she now" spotlight piece it would be an easy excitement. But then I conducted the interview. And in truth, I doubted Prince Henry Charming, now King Charming, would want me to publish what I had seen between him and his wife.

I could still remember Cinderella's tight smile that never reached her eyes, the looming figure of King Charming behind her. The way the interview seemed to go sideways too quickly for me to catch. My cheeks grew warm as I looked away from Red, biting my lip. I hadn't shared my findings. Instead, I had pushed them into a drawer deep within my mind so I could gather my thoughts before I spoke up, but time had clearly run out.

"No," I admitted finally, then quickly added, "I'm hoping to get an outline done today. Did you want to see it before I write?"

Red had practically built the Fairwood Gazette from the ground up, quickly becoming the most respected newspaper in the city. I had curated my writing portfolio for six months before I dared submit my application to her. In truth, I was lucky to get this job, and for the past year, I had learned more than I expected to working under Red. If she wanted something early, I'd make it happen.

But Red leaned back in the old leather chair behind her desk, steepling her fingers. Even though the chair was much too tall for her, she had a presence that filled the room. Making her seem larger than she was.

"I'd like to see the interview," she said.

I sat up. I'd brought a memory project orb to the interview of course—it useful for pulling quotes and reviewing interviews. Using one was like reliving the moment. When you touched the orb, you could smell the same smells, hear the same noises, and see the same things. Anyone looking on could see the images play across the circular sphere and hear what was said.

But Red hadn't asked to see interviews I'd conducted since my very first. I remembered the king listening in on every word Cinderella shared, eyes always watching, hand never leaving the back of her chair. Had I upset him? Was I going to lose my job?

My mouth dried and my pulse quickened as I tried to calmly

say, "Was there a complaint?" Unfortunately, it came out more like a squeak. My hands shook.

Red opened her drawer, placing her personal memory projection orb on the desk in front of me. A muscle in her jaw clenched as she observed me from behind the large orb sitting between us. She seemed pent up, on edge, but something in her eyes softened slightly when she sensed my worry. "No Gretal, you aren't in trouble." Then she gestured to the orb. "If you wouldn't mind?"

I took a deep breath, trying to calm my nerves. What would Red think of the interview? What if she didn't like how I had handled it? The tension within would be undeniable, and I had no doubt an experienced journalist like Red could have smoothed it over better than I had. But I didn't want to deny Red either. Afterall, I hadn't done anything wrong…that I was aware of. And if there was a complaint, Red could see for herself what happened.

So, I stretched my hand forward and touched the orb, recalling the interview in my mind. It projected within the crystal ball, and Red's sharp eyes fixed narrowly on the images forming in front of her.

I was no longer in Red's office, though my body remained there. While Red would watch the memory through the orb, for me, my mind was sucked into the memory, my senses returning to the bright, airy chamber the king's steward led me to for the interview.

"Gretal, I'm so happy you could join us." Cinderella's voice was light, gentle, a whisper of words in a lilted voice. Her hair was still a soft yellow, if a little faded, and her eyes kind as ever though they seemed to reflect a tiredness I couldn't quite place. I wondered if the responsibilities of royalty weighted heavily on our new queen.

I bent my body to bow to her, but she quickly scooped me up

in her arms instead, her hug somehow both firm and soft, her rose scent filling my nose.

I stiffened, surprised by her ease, partially afraid I would ruin her exquisite blue, long sleeved gown if I squeezed her back. But I suppose, only a year ago she was scrubbing dishes and cooking meals for her stepmother and sisters, so she was more one of us commoners than one of the royals.

"Oh, thank you, your majesty," I managed as she stepped back.

"Please, you can just call me Cinderella."

Across the room, someone cleared their throat, and my spine snapped straight when I realized we weren't alone. At the window, King Charming poured himself a drink from a crystalline decanter, his sharp eyes never leaving me and Cinderella. He wore bright red and white, dressed in the colors of his house, and his golden crown glowed atop his head as the sunlight danced across it, mirroring the circlet on Cinderella's brow.

I bowed quickly to him, "Apologizes, your majesty, I didn't expect you'd join us."

The interview was a "where is she now" spotlight piece after the queen's ascent to the throne. I had assumed he would have more important things to do.

He put a stopper in the decanter, sipping the glass filled with a brown liquid before nodding and offering a smile. The corner of his mouth lifted slightly as if tugged by an invisible string. "I simply couldn't miss it." I had only heard his voice when it was booming across the public from his castle balcony. Now, he spoke evenly, his tone deep, his posture sure as he made his way toward us.

"Yes," added Cinderella, "Henry was quite eager to join us today." Something flashed in her eyes, but she turned away too quickly for me to catch it. She gestured to the gilded floral couches in front of the windows. "Please, let's sit."

I followed her quickly, easing myself onto the edge of the couch. The main fabric was white, peppered with pink, red, and yellow roses. The edges and the buttons shone of the same gold as their crowns. I had worn my best clothes to the castle, currently in a brown and green dress with capped sleeves to help the summer heat that suited my pear-shaped frame well. But even though my dress was recently cleaned, it felt too dirty to be on such exquisite furniture.

"Thank you for taking this interview," I started. "The public is eager to learn more about you. Many haven't heard much beyond how you and the king met, and how he scoured the lands for you with only a single shoe to guide him."

Cinderella sat across from me, her gown settling around her like soft sea foam as she folded her hands demurely in her lap. She glanced down through long lashes, a slight blush on her cheeks, as she played with the sleeve at her wrist. "I'm surprised to hear you say that," she said. "I wouldn't think the public would——"

"Nonsense, dear," Henry interrupted. He had walked over to stand behind her, and was now leaning over the couch, catching her chin in his hand.

My eyes lingered on the action, surprised by the possessiveness of it.

Cinderella stiffened as he whispered, "You are a rare jewel. They are right to wonder about you." He tapped a soft kiss to her lips before releasing her jaw and stood back up, his hand on the couch behind her. Wasn't he going to sit down?

Cinderella's blush crept further into her cheeks, giving them a brighter hue. But my eyes lingered on his hand and the way he stood. Calm, yet somehow rigid at the same time. Perhaps he preferred to stand because he had been in many meetings? Afterall, I could only imagine how busy he was running the kingdom. Perhaps he had some unknown stressor bothering him that I—not part of the royals—simply didn't understand.

"What questions do you have for me?" said Cinderella, pulling my eyes away from the king. I had plenty, though admittedly, I hadn't prepared much for them both to answer. I opened my notebook and looked down at the list of questions that were largely lighthearted, focusing on Cinderella's day-to-day life, what she loves most about the castle, her hobbies, how her charity work across the city was going. It was supposed to be a warm article, highlighting the progress of our new queen. With the king here, would my questions be seen as exclusionary? I wondered if I should shift the direction for the king's sake, but Red had tasked me with an interview focused on the queen, so I pressed on.

"Sure, let's start with how you fill your days at the castle?" I said, turning my attention back toward Cinderella.

She toyed with her dress. "Well, typically, I wake up with the sun, then I go cook breakfast in the kitchens."

My brows raised in surprise, and she caught the look as I asked, "You cook breakfast?"

"Well—" Cinderella started.

"She helps the staff," cut in the king, offering a toothy grin as he spoke. "Poor thing couldn't stand sitting on her hands. She even cleans every once in a while too!"

Cinderella's eyes narrowed. The hand in her dress clutched the fabric harder before relaxing as she schooled her face back into the calm demure look she had before.

Behind her, seeming blissfully unaware, the king took a sip of the dark liquid in his glass.

I caught her gaze, unsure of what I had really seen there. Anger? Frustration, maybe? It was gone so quickly.

I looked back at my notebook searching for a question that would lighten the mood. This interview might not be as cut and dry as I had assumed it would be.

"Yes," Cinderella finally broke the silence we'd fallen into. "I do love waking up first thing in the morning and cooking straight away." Her voice was soft and warm, but I detected something false in it.

Above her, the corner of the king's mouth turned down slightly, but otherwise, his composure held.

"I see," I said, trying to break the tension that had quickly filled the room. "And after you cook and eat breakfast, what then?" Though asking about her day was part of the article, I now wanted to know beyond the spotlight. Our new queen had supposedly been lifted out of squalor and abuse by her former stepmother and stepsisters. I had expected to find her happy, relaxed, living her best life. But the woman in front of me was hiding something.

A survivor recognizes a survivor, and something deep within me unfurled. Compelling me to make sure she was okay, to verify that whatever I was seeing wasn't what my gut was warning me against.

In answer to my question, Cinderella cleared her throat and leaned forward, genuine excitement filling her eyes as she said, "Well, typically, I either take a ride on one of our horses, or I embroider with the other ladies at court in the sunroom."

Something in me eased at her sincerity, and I nodded. "How fun. Do you have a favorite horse?"

Queen Cinderella fully smiled now, bright and excited as she thought of her answer. She opened her mouth to speak, but the king cut her off before she could.

"Oh yes, you do love time with your little hobbies," he said with a cocked brow full of arrogance as he added to me, "She'd much prefer to be riding through the flowers than at the council tables."

I did my best to hide my cringe at his words as I eyed Cinderella. She was looking at him calmly, a small smile on her lips. But that smile was nothing like the one she had before when she was going to speak about the horses. My suspicions were confirmed when I eyed her hands, one clutching deep into the folds of her dress. I couldn't see it fully, but I suspected her knuckles were white.

"Isn't that right, dear?" he prompted, turning back to her.

She nodded. Now her smile looked painful. "You know me so well," she murmured.

He chuckled, stepping around the couch to stand closer, now in front of both Cinderella and me. I watched as she released the fabric of her dress, controlling herself even more under his scrutinous eyes. I swallowed, hating what I suspected, that whatever was between them wasn't love. It might have been at one time. But right now, Cinderella looked like a woman trapped in a cage. And I would know, having been trapped in one myself.

"Let's move on," I said, cutting in and offering a smile to try and put her at ease. "You do a considerable amount of charity work, your majesty," I said looking only at her and hoping the king wouldn't cut in this time. "Tell me about the orphanage."

Queen Cinderella glanced at the king first, looking to him for…what? Permission? Or maybe to see if he would interrupt again? Whatever she was searching for seemed to spur her on because she leaned forward. "Oh yes, I love helping where I can. There are so many in need within our kingdom. I work with various charities, but the orphanage must be my favorite."

To my surprise, the King didn't interrupt. In fact, he looked away out the window as she spoke, disinterested.

She tucked a long golden piece of hair behind her ear as she continued. "The castle has so much of everything, I was happy to fill their larder with some of our personal storage."

Suddenly the King's attention was back on Cinderella, his gaze narrowed.

"Wow!" I squeaked, unable to help myself. Both because I was trying to keep the conversation going without him interrupting, and because the scrutiny of his gaze made me want to shrink away. Still though, as one of the kids who had made my way through the orphanage, I knew exactly how in need they were. Winters were hard, and they often only made it through with chicken broth and the occasional loaf of bread. The fact that she had filled their larder meant those children wouldn't feel hunger for the next year or so, and it made me want to hug her.

Unfortunately, the King seemed to have different feelings. I could tell both of us registered the stillness of him as he loomed above us. Somehow, he had become even more rigid as she spoke. Clinging to his glass hard enough that I wondered if he would break it.

The queen glanced up at him, something like satisfaction in her eyes as she did. I couldn't help but feel a rush of pride.

Finally, King Charming snorted dismissively, taking a sip of his drink before saying, "It seems the queen has been even more generous than I knew."

"Very generous," I cut in, drawing her attention back to me. I leaned closer. "Tell me, do you have any big future plans on the horizon?"

This time, the King didn't even let her start to answer. "Soon we will fill this castle with children. Won't we, dearest?" Now it was his turn to look satisfied as Cinderella nodded stiffly, struggling to keep her smile plastered on her lips.

My heart sank, my eyes flicking away from her and to the King, who was paying no mind to me as he eyed his wife with a smugness that I wanted to wipe off his face. Defeat, anger, sadness all seemed to be gathering in Cinderella's eyes as she took a moment to gather herself while eyeing the windows.

It was then I realized that, despite the stifling summer heat, she was wearing a long-sleeved dress. Even now, she tugged at the sleeve, and I could see small beads of sweat forming on her brow. That dress looked heavy. It was clearly not made for the warm months. Why would she wear a dress like that this time of year? My mouth went dry, and my heart thumped in my ears as I realized why any woman might do exactly that.

Was she hiding bruises? The thought crashed over me with such force it rendered me speechless. I hoped I was wrong. Yet, in my gut, I knew I likely wasn't.

What article could I possibly write now? If I shared exactly what I was seeing, if the people of the kingdom knew, would things get better for her? Or…as they sadly usually did, would they get worse?

And what if I was wrong? If I published something that was negative, only to have her come out and say she had no idea why I would say such things, what would happen then? I could lose my job. Or get thrown in the dungeon if the king was angry enough. Not to mention what it might do to the Fairwood Gazette's reputation.

I swallowed hard, unsure what to do next. Unsure of if I should, or if I even could, help.

The thick silence around us broke as a steward rushed in, the buttons of his tight-fitting shirt stretched over a round belly as he quickly bowed, "Your majesties, my apologies for the interruption. We had an urgent matter at council. Could you join us, my king?"

Hope skittered down my spine, and I sat straighter as I realized I might be left alone with the queen. I could ask her what was going on, get to the bottom of this. I could even ask her how she wanted me to publish the article. If she needed or wanted my help.

She looked at me as well, our gaze meeting while the king was distracted, as if we were conspirators sharing a secret. Did she hope for the same thing? There seemed to be a new light in her eyes.

King Charming smiled, putting down his crystal cup on one of the gilded side tables with a clink. "Of course, Dorin." Then turning towards me, he said, "We'll have to call it for today. So glad you came by."

The light in Cinderella's eyes quickly died as my hope dropped to the floor like a stone.

"Oh," I stuttered. "I do have a few more questions for the queen?"

I chewed my lip, wishing I hadn't sounded so desperate. I wanted to make sure she was safe, to see if she needed help, to ask her exactly what she wanted me to put in this article. But the king only shook his head, slamming the door of possibility closed as he said, "Sorry, the queen is needed in council as well. Come, dear." He waited for her by the door.

Queen Cinderella stood up and brushed herself off slowly. Her throat bobbed as she swallowed hard. I stood when she did, eyeing her, looking for some sign that she wanted me to stay. But then what I would do? Standing up to the king wasn't exactly within my capability. But if she needed help, I wasn't about to leave her.

Instead, she came over to me and wrapped me in a gentle hug, pulling me close.

Over her shoulder, I could see the king focused on us through narrowed eyes.

I wanted to whisper and ask if she was okay. But with his eyes on us, I didn't dare. I clenched my jaw, paralyzed with indecision.

She pulled back, keeping her hands on my shoulders, and offered me a soft, genuine smile. "Thank you, Gretal, for coming. It was so good to see you. I hope all is well with your family. And please do give Red my best."

Before I could say anything, she swept away, gliding towards the king.

I quickly bowed to them both, a lump forming in my throat. Something had just slipped through my fingers, and I wasn't sure how to get it back. A pit in my stomach yawned open, and I felt as helpless as I had been when I was young, begging the witch to stop stuffing my brother in the stove.

"Dorin, show the reporter out, please," said King Charming with a dismissive wave of his hand as he led Queen Cinderella out of the room, his palm firmly on the small of her back.

I watched after them, for several moments, before Red's voice echoed in my head.

"Alright, I've seen enough."

I pulled my hand from the orb, and blinked, reorienting myself back in Red's office. Beside us, the fire continued to roar, and Red gazed at it, one hand under her chin as she contemplated what she had seen. Her brows scrunched together with worry.

My gut twisted as I waited for her reaction. I should have done something more. My fingers ached to write a scathing article that damned the king, but my gut told me that was a bad idea. For me. For the Gazette. And likely, for Cinderella, which had held me perpetually frozen, unable to write a single word on the page.

"As you can see the interview was…" I struggled to find the words.

Red waved a hand, stopping me. Just looking at her face told me she was just as worried for the queen as I was.

She sighed as she stood, running a hand through her long scarlet hair as she moved toward the fire, leaning against the exposed brick. I wondered if watching that interview had done for her what it had for me. Perhaps it reminded us both of a darker time.

"You haven't written any of that down?" she asked, glancing back at me.

"No," I admitted, "I wasn't sure how to…shape it." I checked that the door to her office was still closed and leaned forward, dropping my voice. Perhaps Red could give me clarity on what to write. "Do you think, that maybe, I should write what I saw? Exactly what I saw?"

She looked back at the fire for a long moment before answering. "No."

The chair scraped the floor as I stood before my mind registered the movement, "We can't just pretend she is okay!" It was the most forceful I had been with Red, but I didn't regret the words. Yes, I was struggling with what to write. But Red and I had been through too much in our own lives to turn away when we saw clear signs of abuse. We could practically still feel the scraping of claws and knives against our skin. We had lingering bruises, even though we healed long ago.

To my dismay, she shook her head again. Her red hair waving around her throat as she did. "We aren't going to write the article at all." There was a finality in her voice. An expectation to listen, but I wasn't ready to let it go just yet.

"Red," I said through gritted teeth. "Why wouldn't we write something. We can't just abandon her." I refused to believe Red would turn a blind eye to this. Had the king threatened her? Or had Cinderella made some kind of request? There had to be something more at play here.

She glanced back at me and must have read my shock and disappointment because her gaze hardened, and I remembered how on edge she had been before I showed her that memory.

Her shoulders tense, that muscle in her jaw ticking as she ground her teeth.

"The king was found dead this morning. He won't be a problem for her anymore."

I recoiled, both relief and horror flooding through me. "What?" I managed. "What happened?"

Fire returned to Red's eyes. "Apparently there was poison in his breakfast."

Fair and Balanced

Logan Sidwell

A gently curving valley of pre-planned sidewalks, roads, and houses paved over a swamp. The fees were high, the rules were strict, and the lawn edging was perfect. The grass didn't dare risk a fine for trespassing on the sidewalk. In the boiling heat of the afternoon, a rusted, dark blue 2009 Dodge Avenger rattled past the gates and to a stop at the first intersection of Blue Sky Docks.

"You know you can run those." Perry fumbled with the device in his hands.

Sean glanced in both directions and pressed the gas. Acceleration came, albeit a half second slow. "Stop signs are there for a reason, man. I stop and someone else goes. It's balanced. What if a kid comes running out?"

Perry wiped the sweat from his brow, raised his device to the window, and pointed it at the nearest house. "A kid's not gonna be out here in this heat. At least do a rolling stop. I don't want to be here any longer than we have to. The charges for burglarizing are way bigger than running a stop sign. These houses are all cold—take us to the next street."

The rusty Dodge Avenger rounded a corner and started down the next line of houses. Sean tilted his head to see the display on Perry's device. The thermal scanner outputted a blurry red-and-blue outline of the neighborhood. Every house was colored a similar dark blue.

"Eyes on the road, man."

Sean turned forward and straightened up. "Sorry, I didn't want to miss the moment."

"It's just a house with the air conditioning turned off. You're not missing anything."

House after house, the scanner showed an ocean-blue outline. All they needed to find was the one in the bunch with an orange outline. The idea had come up during a lengthy discussion on the punitive and legal differences between burglary and robbery. Folks on vacation turned off their A/C in the summer. Thus, the search for the hot house in a cold neighborhood. Finding the thermal scanner at a pawn shop was a bit of serendipity, though the purchase had emptied both their bank accounts.

"Got one." It didn't quite look orange, but the yellowish silhouette on the screen was far hotter than the rest of the neighborhood.

Sean turned into the driveway of 3048 S Tidal Street. The townhouse's white and teal paint job was identical to its neighbors', with the exception of a crack in the pavement in front of the light-oak door. He had done a couple burglaries in the past, but never somewhere so nice. "Don't places like this have tons of cameras?"

"Only at the gates. Nothing to worry about." Perry pushed open his door and hopped onto the pavement. Sean made no move to follow, content to watch his shorter friend jog up the driveway and around the corner on his own. Something about this place bothered him. Maybe it was the perfect way every house led into the next, or the precisely edged lawns that all had a mailbox on the same corner. A place this pretty needed something ugly to balance it out, or at least something a little asymmetrical. They'd need to move quickly—a pair of mid-20s guys in ratty shoes and torn jeans wouldn't have to do much to stand out around here.

Perry returned at an awkward half-jogging, half-walking gait. His mouth was pressed oddly flat, but the corners kept twitching. Sean shut off the engine and undid his seatbelt in anticipation of the news.

"Door's unlocked, let's go."

Concerns or no, when it was time to go, you go. Two seconds was the difference between a clean escape and a cop's hand catching your hoodie and dragging you down off the fence. Sean knew that feeling all too well. He matched Perry's half-running pace the whole way up the driveway and into the house.

The temperature inside wasn't much hotter than the boiling roads outside, but the thermal scanner had failed to mention the humidity. The place was like a sauna; every breath coated Sean's lungs with tulip-scented air. Sean's body swayed unsteadily, and he reached for the wall. Something brushed against his fingers and shattered against the floor.

"Careful!" Perry hissed.

Sean scanned the hall. Knick-knacks, clocks, dolls, and photos were layered over each other on every wall. Only an inch of bare paint sat above a broken frame and shattered glass. He picked the picture up and set it on a nearby desk. The wrinkled lady in the photo reminded him of his Nana back when he was a kid— the whole place did. All that was missing was the cookies. If he had the tape, he would have put the glass back himself. It wasn't fair to both burglarize the place and leave a mess. By the time Sean had caught his footing, Perry was halfway up the stairs to the second floor. "Perry!" He whisper-yelled.

Perry didn't bother turning. "What?"

"This is some old lady's place. We're wasting our time."

Perry waved him to follow. "There's always something. Jewelry and collectibles, keep an eye out for jewelry and collectibles."

The pair padded up the stairs, their feet sinking deeper into the carpet with each step. At the top, a thin hallway led past four doors to a washer and dryer at the back.

"I'll take one side, you take the other," Perry said as pushed open the first door on the left. He froze. "Shit."

Perry's horrified, frowning expression was very much like the one Sean had seen back when Perry realized that all his drinking and shouting was taking place in the middle of a cop bar. A sign of bad things. Sean inched closer, curious to see what had spooked his partner. Past Perry's shoulder, there was an old bed layered in pastel quilts, a finely carved dresser, the body of an old woman on the rug, and a striped flower and herb wallpaper. "I thought the place was empty."

"Me too." Perry answered.

"But the A/C was off."

"She's a grandma. Grandmas would live in a furnace if they could. It's probably what did her in." Perry took one deep breath, then stepped over the woman's legs and into the room. "Come on, let's get to work."

Sean asked, "Does that make this a robbery?"

Perry pulled open a drawer. "Not when she's already dead. Go check the other rooms."

Sean took a moment to observe the old woman. She wore a pink dress and soft cotton slippers. Her wrinkled face bore a tranquil expression. At that age, when death came, it was probably just a quiet farewell. No suffering, just a quick goodbye. She wouldn't miss a few belongings. Maybe her vulture kids might, but she wouldn't. She had already taken everything her soul could balance to the other side. Before Perry got annoyed, Sean turned around and pushed open a door across the way.

Looked like a craft studio. There was a clay mold on the table, some vials on the shelves at the back, and a surprising number of wires in the drawers. She must have hopped between projects a lot. Regardless, not much of value. Sean hurried to the next room.

Another bedroom, probably a guest. Compared to the rest of the house, the decorations here were downright minimal. The bed was topped by a simple comforter. The dressers and night-stands were what you could buy at Ikea. Sean went through the drawers and closet as quickly as he could, pausing only to look at a photo on a nightstand. The dead woman stood with a group of men and women in their late 20s, kids probably. It must have been a special occasion. Every one of them wore black, and their smiles were slight.

"Sean! Get in here!"

Sean hurried back to the bedroom. Perry only used that voice when there was a really big screw-up.

He found Perry standing near the old woman's head, holding a box of jewelry but staring down at the body.

"What's up?"

"I need you to think very carefully, Sean. Were this lady's eyes always open?"

The tranquil expression on the old woman's face was long gone. Her chest slowly rose and fell, and her thick eyebrows and wide-eyed look expressed what could only be fury.

"So, this is a robbery," Sean whispered. Three times the pris-on sentence and twice the guilt knowing they were stealing from someone who would miss their belongings. They couldn't pos-sibly rob the whole place now. Perry backed away towards the door. The woman's gaze followed him with every step. Maybe he could be convinced to leave some of it behind.

"No shit, it's a robbery. We need to finish the job and get out. Check the other room. I'll keep an eye on her."

Sean paused. His own Nana had passed away so suddenly, no one had even realized she was gone for four days. Even a minute at a hospital bed to say goodbye would have meant the world. "Shouldn't we call someone?"

Perry's eyebrows lowered and he spoke in a deeper register. "Are you trying to get us arrested?"

They had arguments like this from time to time. Sean always lost.

He looked at the old woman. She deserved another chance. "Maybe we were sent here for a reason, ya know? Maybe this is our path, to save this lady's life rather than taking her stuff."

The intensity in Perry's eyes softened to annoyance. "How about this: the lady was going to die, right?"

"Right."

"So now we're saving her. But in exchange, she loses a few valuables. Sort of a divine trade. You'd give up a couple rings and necklaces for a second chance at life, wouldn't you?"

Sean leaned against the door frame. He had heard of the old "coins for the ferryman" story. How many coins did it cost to reschedule your death for later in the year? The old woman's eyes jumped to Sean. If this was a stroke, they'd need to call an ambulance sooner rather than later.

"That seems fair." Sean turned quickly and hurried to the last door. The room was unfinished, with a bare wood floor, unfinished walls, and pipes going in every direction. Not likely to find much, but Perry wouldn't take that for an answer. Sean fished out his phone and flipped on the light. A couple dozen glossy black plastic chairs shined in the dark, more than enough for a thanksgiving dinner. Beyond the chairs, tucked in a corner, a stack of boxes kept to themselves.

Sean pushed through the chairs to the boxes in the corner, pulling the first from the stack. It weighed heavy in his hands. He peeled back the cardboard flaps and glanced inside. A gun. That wasn't right. Sean pointed his phone into the box to illuminate the contents. Definitely a gun. A stack of passports lay next to the weapon on a bed of cash. From the weight of the box, this wasn't just savings for a rainy day.

Sean balanced the first box on the nearby chairs and went for the next. This one was even heavier. Four different colors of currency were reflected by the phone's light, although Sean only recognized the dollars. The next two boxes were just cash. More than he had ever seen in his life, enough to fund years on the road. At least Perry would be happy. Sean carried the first box back to the bedroom. Perry was sitting on the bed tapping the old woman's jewelry box with his fingers.

"I found something."

Perry perked up. "Really?"

Sean tilted the contents towards Perry. Perry raised the gun out of the box. The two wordlessly shared a look, then turned to the woman on the floor.

"You're no regular old woman, are you?"

The old woman blinked. Perry jumped to his feet.

"There's three more boxes," said Sean.

Perry's eyes lit up. "I'll grab 'em."

Sean followed his partner to the door, then cast a final glance back at the old woman. Whoever she was, or used to be, she deserved better than to be left on the floor to rot. "We're gonna call an ambulance, right?"

Perry was halfway down the stairs when he answered. "Huh? Yeah. Sure, once we're out of here."

"That'll make it even, right?"

Perry grunted under the weight of tens of thousands of dollars and a small box of jewelry. "One criminal life saved for a couple hundred thousand dollars? What can be more even than that?"

Sean hurried down the stairs to follow him. Something about

the deal still felt wrong. "So, the lady's even, I get that. Are we even?"

"What do you mean?"

"Well, we got the jewelry for saving a life. What did we do to deserve a hundred thousand dollars?"

Perry balanced his boxes on one leg, an annoyed expression on his face. "We've had it rough in life. This is probably the universe's way of paying us back."

That didn't seem quite balanced either. He hadn't done enough good in his life to justify something like this. "I don't think that's enough, man. We need to pay the universe back."

Perry lowered his boxes to the floor and stared daggers at Sean. "What do you propose?"

"Break my foot."

"What?"

"It's something negative enough to justify getting the money. Break my foot, then I'll break yours."

"You want me to break your foot?" Perry's eyes narrowed.

"Yeah."

"Okay." Perry grasped the edges of the table near the door, lifted it, lined up one of the legs with Sean's foot, then glanced at Sean.

"Come on!"

Perry shrugged and brought the leg down hard.

Sean fell to the floor. The pain was a screaming, all-encompassing thing that dominated his every thought. He couldn't focus his eyes. Perry had performed his role to perfection. The foot was undoubtedly broken. At the edge of his consciousness, he could tell Perry had gone outside with the boxes. After a minute, the flood of sensation began to dull, and Sean dragged himself up onto his one good leg.

The front door opened again a moment later, and with Perry's help, Sean hopped his way back to the car. Through labored breaths, Sean spoke. "So when do you want me to break your foot? When we get back?"

Perry gave no answer except to help Sean into the passenger seat before climbing into the driver's seat. Sean glanced in the back. Four boxes filled with cash were tucked in front of the seats, and a jewelry box lay loose on the chair. "Can we leave the jewelry? We're already taking a fortune, taking extra seems petty."

Perry sneered. "That doesn't sound even to me."

The engine sputtered to life and reversed out of the driveway. It wasn't long before Sean was watching the Blue Sky Docks shrink away in the rearview mirror. A sick feeling settled into his stomach.

"We need to call an ambulance for that lady," Sean muttered. His partner gave no reaction. With every turn, the unpleasantness deepened. There was a cold, determined look in Perry's eyes Sean had never seen before. Soon enough they were passing the city bus station.

"Pull over here."

"What for?"

"I want to get out."

Perry set his jaw. The car continued its regular trajectory. After a couple seconds, Sean spoke again. "Please?"

Perry sighed, and the car began to decelerate then stopped.

Sean stepped out and hopped to the back. Under Perry's watchful eye, he retrieved two of the old woman's cartons from the back, careful to avoid the jewelry box on the seat. Sean placed his boxes on the ground and waved to Perry. Without a word, Perry sped off down the road. Just as Perry always did, he ran through a stop sign.

He never saw the ten-ton greyhound bus coming.

Ten tons of weight crashed through the driver's side of the Avenger. In an instant, the vehicle's width was halved. What was left behind sped another 50 feet down the road, flipping, rolling, and shedding pieces all along the way. When it came to a stop, the car was nothing but scrap metal and hundred-dollar bills flying in the wind.

Sean took a deep, shaky breath. Perry had been a friend for a long time, although he wasn't always the kindest. If he was alive, he'd probably be stuck in a hospital bed staring up at others for months. If he was alive, Sean would visit him. But there was something else that needed to be done first. Without a moment's pause, Sean picked up his boxes, hopped in a circle, and made for the payphone in the corner. He had a call to make.

About the Authors

Eric John Anderson is an award-winning author and screenwriter from Utah. He has lived on both coasts, but he finds the most peace when lost deep in the mountain wilderness. When he's not writing queer literary fiction or supernatural horror, he's playing intense strategy board games or explaining obscure films to uninterested friends.

Born and raised in the mountainous state of Colorado, **Jacob Badger** is the third child of the family, appropriately born in the Chinese Year of the Monkey. Growing up in the early 90s, he spent most of his free time watching The Lion King, Jurassic Park, DragonHeart, and Stars Wars. These stories would give him an intense love of the scientific, the cosmological, and the fantastical at an early age and would inspire many stories of faraway worlds, the magic of scientific knowledge, and nonhuman characters when he started writing. Now returned to the promised land of South Jordan, Utah, he spends his time as a favored uncle to his two nieces and two nephews.

Scott Bryan is the author of the Foresight Chronicles series. Currently he's spending a lot of time as the scribe for a three-hundred-year-old vampire child, sharing tales of her endless battles with Dracula across history. He also searches the Multiverse, looking for fascinating narratives to share with this world. He's met lost fantasy creatures, demonic beings, time travelers, and Multiversal agents, each of whom have offered him stories to tell. When not creating worlds, Scott generates technical drawings, enjoys life with his wife and children, collects stories and figures of heroic champions, and walks his fierce warrior Chihuahua. Scott is a member of the League of Utah Writers, Infinite Monkey division. You can find him on the web at http://authorfcscott.wixsite.com/authorfcscott

Emmeline de Vere is a recovering lawyer who has lived in California, England, Israel, and now calls Utah home. Her fantasy romance novel A Season of Shades is being released serially at emmelinedevere.com, where she also blogs her discoveries in Victorian etiquette and ancient demonology.

Sara Fitzgerald is an award-winning, multi-published author. She usually writes romance novels, as well as young adult paranormal novels and hopeful Christmas stories, but recently, she has discovered she loves to write scary stories. Sara has won numerous awards, including the Writer of the Year from the League of Utah Writers in 2006. Recently, she won the prestigious Silver Quill Award from the League of Utah Writers in 2024 for her Novella A Kiss for Kate. She won first place in the horror category in the Eagle Mountain Writing Contest in 2025. Sara makes her home in Salt Lake City with her husband, daughter, and their zany American Eskimo dog, Glitter. She loves writing, watercolor painting, and spending time with her family.

Jayrod Garrett believes in working towards a world where all of us can feel we belong. They are a storytelling educator with a Master of Fine Arts in Creative Writing from the University of Nevada, Reno. As a child, they came to Utah on a three-week vacation that became more than forty years. During that time, they transitioned from being a faithful member of the Church of Jesus Christ of Latter-Day Saints into a nonbinary, Black, atheist, U.S. Veteran with PTSD and ADHD. Currently they are a ghostwriter with Super Huemann Creative, an educator for RISE Virtual Academy where they teach Black students about Black history, a storyteller with the Nubian Storytellers of Utah Leadership, a Game Master running role playing games at Salt Lake City's Legendarium, and the Belonging Coordinator of Superstars Writing Seminars. They live in northern Utah with their spouse and three children. You can find more on their stories, poetry, and where they are teaching at jayrodpgarrett.com.

Gina G grew up in sunny St George, Utah, where the "summer sun spends the winter." After a brief stint in Idaho, Gina G found herself in Washington State, where she fell in love with the trees, the rain, the people, and Seattle. After 23 years, life and circumstances brought her back to her hometown. She is learning to love red rocks, but every day… she misses the rain. Gina G is the author of Secrets Café, an LGBTQ three-part spicy love story set in Seattle. Book 1: The Appetizer and Book 2: The Main Course are available at Amazon.com and Barnes and Noble. Book 3: Just Desserts is at the publishers. She won a Quills Bronze Typewriter award for her short story, "Culling the Humans." You can follow her on Facebook at Gina Gauthor, on Instagram at @ginagauthors, and on Twitter at @author_ginag.

Danielle Harward is a professional ghostwriter who writes fantasy and horror in her personal time. Her short stories have won several awards and have been published in over ten anthologies. She loves to paint, shoot arrows, and chat about her bird. And as someone who typically writes over 50,000 words a month, some wonder if she is clinically insane.

Inna Lyon, a Russian bumpkin, was raised on a steady diet of cabbage and potatoes, along with the required reading of Chekhov and Dostoevsky. During the day, she works as an accountant, specializing in colorful aging reports and cute collection letters. At night, Lyon writes stories about life, miracles, and cats. A member of the League of Utah Writers, she participates in the Infinite Monkeys, and she currently serves as president of the Blue Quill Chapter. An award-winning writer in various genres, Lyon writes in both English and Russian. She lives in Utah with her big, happy family.

Makayla Nielson was raised in Normal, Illinois and currently resides in Lehi, Utah with her husband and three children. When she's not writing, she's out on adventures in the canyons near her home, watching science fiction movies, or crocheting (always with a snack or two within reach). She is currently the Contest Committee Chair for The League of Utah Writers and has written short stories for Flash Fiction Magazine, Balloons Lit. Journal, Inkpot Literary Magazine, Stance: Studies on the Family, and Manawaker Studios Flash Fiction Podcast. Find her at: https://makaylanielson.com/

Pat Partridge writes across genres. He is the author of the mystery Fragile Memories, the sequel, Buried at Bears Ears, and the humorous road-trip novel Fast on Fifty. His book of political humor is now in its third edition. Over the past three years, he has won eleven awards from the League of Utah Writers for his short fiction and novel first chapters. Recently, his short fiction has appeared in Remington Review, The Haven, Fabula Argentea, Ariel Chart, Litro, and multiple anthologies. He is pleased others find his writing worth reading.

Talysa Sainz is a freelance editor and award-winning author who believes life's deepest truths can be found in fiction. She runs her own editing business and spends her time at the library or volunteering with the League of Utah Writers. Always fascinated with the structure of words, she studied English Linguistics and Editing at BYU. She then went on to receive a Master of Science in Management and Leadership, focusing on nonprofit work, from WGU. Talysa is the President of the Utah Freelance Editors.

Alexander Self is a woman who has massive dreams but microscopic follow-through. She's still new to the writing game, so she hopes her work delights you. If not, keep it to yourself. With a face that her mother can tolerate, she enjoys learning and has taken classes in things such as mermaid swimming and diving, Australian didgeridoo, natural perfume making, pilates on a paddleboard, screenwriting, a sci-fi and fantasy workshop, a horror writing bootcamp, zen lessons for writers, camp cooking, and much more. She is the second-time winner of "tackiest tourist" costume contests and continues to blind passersby with her mayo complexion skin. See if one day you find her shoveling sweets down her gullet, and maybe you'll be able to hear her beyond cringy puns. Now if you'll excuse her, she has to go be stupid somewhere else.

Logan Sidwell is a sci-fi writer, coder, and puzzle-maker from Utah. He got his start in writing by simulating starships, then went on to design education simulations with mission.io, he strives to marry his background in Computer Science and his years of storytelling to create fun, compelling ideas that explore new ground in technological and fantastical settings.

Fred Smullin a writer passionate about exploring human connection and the transformative journeys that shape us. He's spent 35 years writing software in the private and public sectors and international consulting. For the past decade, his side gig as a progressive Christian lay pastor has enabled him to draw deeply from his recovery and spiritual growth journey. Once an addict, he now embraces a life shaped by faith, grace, and a profound connection to his Higher Power. He enjoys hiking, cooking, fantasizing about retirement, and relaxing when not writing.

Sobey Snow is an artist, who enjoys exploring the worlds of fiction and music. Coming from Ogden, Utah, Sobey earns his living by mentoring youths with special needs and spends his free time practicing his craft. Sobey is a proud member of the League of Utah Writers, Infinite Monkeys chapter. www.sobeysnow.com

Thomas I. Wahl is a Quills award-winning author. Following his retirement, he has dedicated himself to creative writing, specializing in short stories and historical fiction informed by his agricultural experiences in Northwest Iowa and his family history. Wahl and his wife live in Salt Lake City, where he enjoys photography, brewing beer, making BBQ sauces/rubs, and dog treats.

Johnny Worthen is a widely published, award-winning, best-selling author of books and stories. Trained in stand-up comedy, modern literary criticism and cultural studies, he writes excellent multi-genre fiction, symbolized by his love of tie-dye and good words. "I wear tie-dye for my friends, but I write what I like to read," he says. "This guarantees me at least one fan and easy dressing decisions in the morning." Johnny teaches writing at the University of Utah and lives in a house with his wife, assorted cats. There's also a lawn. Find him at: www.johnnyworthen.com.

Rashelle Yeates is a horticulturist who loves growing plants as well as seeing them grow, especially in their native habitats. This has led to a love of traveling, experiencing as many different cultures as she can and bringing that joy and experience into her writing.

Daniel Yocom writes about geeky things because people say to write what you know. Their love of the geeky, nerdy community dates to the 1960s through games, books, movies, and stranger things better shared in small groups. They're an award-winning writer and editor of short stories, books, and hundreds of articles published by blogs, magazines, and gaming companies. They enjoy attending conferences, conventions, and festivals and sharing on panels and presentations. They are serving on the boards of the LTUE Writing Symposium and the League of Utah Writes as the president of the Infinite Monkeys Genre Writers Chapter. They also serve on the Selection and Awards juries for the FilmQuest Film Festival and as the Panel Coordinator for the SaltCON Tabletop Gaming Convention. Dan wants to help others reach their goals as creative people. Join them at www.guildmastergaming.com.

Postscript

Rachael Bush

The League of Utah Writers was founded in 1935 and has spent the last ninety years empowering the writing and publishing goals of its members. We aim to be the most sought after, accessible, and inclusive writing organization in Utah. One of the ways that goal is accomplished is through the varied writing chapters that span the state of Utah.

The Infinite Monkeys are more than just a chapter of the League of Utah Writers. In the last nine years, they have built a close-knit community. And when things feel bleak, it is this community that creates hope for us all.

Rachael Bush
President for the League of Utah Writers